B

Harbour

A Detective Hodgins Victorian Mystery

Nanci M. Pattenden, PLCGS

Murder Does Pay, Ink

This is a work of fiction. All characters, names, incidents, organizations, and dialogue in this novel are either the products of the author's imagination or are used fictitiously.

Published by Murder Does Pay, Ink
Ontario, Canada
www.murderdoespayink.ca

The views expressed in this work are solely those of the author and do not necessarily reflect the views of the publisher, and the publisher hereby disclaims any responsibility for then.

ISBN 978-0-9918979-5-7 (print)

Detective Hodgins Victorian Murder Mysteries

Body in the Harbour

Death on Duchess Street

ACKNOWLEDGMENTS

A huge thank you to my editor, Melissa Moores of Infinite Pathways. Her expertise and suggestions were much appreciated.

A big thanks also goes out to my 'Graphics Guru' Christopher Watts. You did a fantastic job.

CHAPTER 1

Danny stretched out on his belly half way up Conner's Wharf watching the ice swirl, while Michael stood at the end of the wharf, throwing snowballs at the seagulls as they flew overhead, screeching their displeasure. Waves thrashed the pilings of the wharf, churning chunks of ice around Toronto Harbour. Several pieces surrounded something soft, grinding against it; pushing it further into the hard sand along the waterfront.

"Hey Mikey, what's that?"

Michael walked over to Danny and knelt beside him. He turned his head, following Danny's outstretched arm, and shrugged. Danny scrambled to his feet. "Looks like someone threw out some old clothes. Let's go see."

Danny ran back along the wharf with Michael following slowly, not terribly interested in a pile of clothing. Jumping down near the shoreline, Danny slipped on the rocks. His shoe hit the cold water, instantly soaking his foot. Michael hurried to his brother's side and helped him up. Making their way towards the shoreline, Michael stopped and grabbed his little brother's arm.

"It's not clothes," Michael said.

Danny pulled away from his brother's grip and moved in for a closer look. "I never saw a dead man before," he said reaching out.

Michael grabbed hold of the back of Danny's coat. "Don't touch it. We'd better get Dad."

They scrambled to the road, and ran up Lorne Street to the Queen's Hotel on Front. The doorman smiled and gave his usual greeting to the two boys who'd become regulars at the hotel over the Christmas break.

"Good day Master Daniel, Master Michael."

Instead of stopping to chat, they headed straight to the front desk looking for their father, Ben Grove, manager of the hotel. Between gulps of air they told him about the man on the shore. Ben had trouble understanding, but once they calmed down and got their breath back, he had them repeat everything. He found it difficult to believe his sons had actually stumbled across a dead body, but their wide eyes and shaky voices told him something was definitely wrong.

Two of Ben's oldest friends were in the dining room arguing about the local politics and enjoying the hotel's signature dish, Fillets of beef a la Rossine. Ben took

Michael and Danny over to their table.

"Sam, Charlie, sorry to interrupt, but I need your help." Ben repeated the boy's story. "Can they sit with you while I fetch the police?"

"You sure he's dead?" Charlie asked. "Might be some drunk still celebrating the new year."

"No, I don't think so, Mr. Kelly," Michael said. "He looked like the dead fox we found by the pond last summer." Michael looked at Danny and made a face. "Except the man didn't smell bad."

The two men agreed to sit with the boys. As Ben hurried out, he stopped to ask a waiter to bring some hot tea for them. He headed out the front door and sprinted along Front Street in the direction of Number Four station on Wilton Avenue. As he crossed Bay Street, he noticed a young policeman making his rounds. Ben stopped him and repeated what his boys said. The constable blew his whistle and a few minutes later, a heavy set constable came huffing around the corner from Wellington Street and joined them. They spoke for a moment, then 'Tubby' headed east towards the station. The first constable introduced himself as Henry Barnes and asked Ben to take him to the boys.

When they arrived back at the Queens, Michael and Danny told Barnes where they found the body. Barnes pulled a pencil out of one pocket, a receipt out of another, and then made a few notes on the back.

"Probably drunk and fell off the pier." He put the paper back into his pocket. "Can you show me exactly where this alleged body is?" Ben and Constable Barnes followed the boys down Lorne Street, their overshoes sloshing in the melted snow. As soon as they spotted the body, Ben sent Danny and Michael home.

It was just as the boys had described. The man was face down, half on the beach, half in the water. His arms were covered in sand and snow. The bottom edge of a long dark overcoat fanned out around the body's legs. Several seagulls pecked at his head, pulling off small bits of skin and hair. Most of the birds flew off when the men ran towards the shoreline, but a few lingered a couple of feet away, as though waiting for the intruders to leave.

"Bloody birds. You'd think they were vultures instead of gulls. Don't suppose the poor sot cares though, eh Constable?" Ben grabbed a handful of snow, formed a ball and threw it at the birds. It exploded when it hit the ground and the remaining gulls flew off.

Ben turned around when he received no answer. Barnes was standing a few feet back, staring at the dead man. All the colour had drained from his face.

"We can't just leave him there," Ben said. "Help me drag him the rest of the way out of the water. Constable!

Pull yourself together. Grab his arm. He can't harm you." Ben moved behind Barnes and gave him a little shove. Barnes stumbled towards the body and stopped.

"Looks like the waves and ice have partially buried him. We'll have to free him up from the sand first." Ben used his hands to move the cold, heavy sand off the dead man's arms so they could get a good grip. He reached under the stiff's right armpit and told the constable to grab the left. Barnes obediently did as he was told, and together they dragged the corpse a few feet up the frozen shore. The head had turned. Barnes looked down at his face, let go of the arm, ran under the pier and threw up.

Ben looked down the shoreline and spotted the Yacht Club in the distance. "Wait here," he said, and sprinted to the club. He returned ten minutes later with a tarp and a well-worn blanket. He dropped the tarp on the ground and placed the blanket over the corpse. He noticed Barnes had not moved from the edge of the pier and was staring at the lifeless form. Ben walked over to him and placed his hand on the constable's shoulder.

"How long have you been on the force?"

"Three months, Sir."

"Shouldn't you get someone with a little more experience to help with this?"

With the body covered and out of sight, the constable

started to regain his composure. "I sent Constable Snider to get a senior office and the coroner. They should be here any time."

The sound of voices drifted down from the street above. "There they are now. Looks like one of the detectives with the coroner," Barnes said, waving his arms at the two men approaching in a buggy. They stopped the buggy at the end of Lorne Street and tied the horses to a post. The two men crossed Esplanade, then the train tracks and walked down to the edge of the pier. The shorter man carried a doctor's bag, so Ben figured the tall one must be the detective. The contrast between the two men was almost comical. The coroner was short and heavy set; his coat fit so tight it looked like it would burst open. His flaming orange sideburns stood out dramatically against his pale skin, even from a distance. The detective was at least twenty years younger, tall and lanky. His overcoat was open, revealing a suit that looked tailor made. He took long strides, and walked with an air of confidence; the doctor had to trot to keep up.

Hodgins looked at the covered body, nodded, then said, "Guess that's him then. He's all yours Doctor."

Dr. McKenzie was sweating, even though the temperature had steadily dropped over the past few hours. He took a hanky out of his coat pocket, and wiped his brow before kneeling down beside the corpse.

Hodgins buttoned his overcoat as he looked around. "I was told a couple of boys found the body. Where are they?"

"Yes, my sons. I didn't want them here any longer than necessary.

Hodgins glared at Barnes. "I hope you at least spoke to them."

"Yes, Sir," Barnes stammered. "I interviewed them at the hotel before they showed me the body. They don't know much. Just found him when they were playing."

"Right." Hodgins turned to Ben. "And who are you?"

"Ben Grove. Manager at the Queen's Hotel."

"Do you recognize the dead man?"

"Don't think so, but it's hard to tell."

"Hard to tell? Why? Either you know him or you don't."

"Take a look at him Detective. You'll see."

"The man's right," Dr. McKenzie said. "Even his mother would have trouble identifying him."

McKenzie lifted the blanket. "The whole left side is scraped down to the bone. What's left of the skin is barely hanging on."

"I figure it's from the ice in the harbour," Ben said. "Don't think he's been in there long though. I've seen people pulled from the water before. He's not all bloated like you'd expect."

"This where you found him?"

"Not exactly," Ben said. "Didn't seem right to leave him there, what with the gulls pecking at him and all. I got the constable to help me pull him out of the water. The blanket's from the Yacht Club. It's always left open in case of emergencies."

"You shouldn't have moved the body. You've disturbed any evidence that might have been around." Hodgins scowled at Barnes. "You should have known better."

The constable opened his mouth to say something but the glare from Hodgins stopped him.

Hodgins continued, "I can see from the drag marks just how far you moved him. Wouldn't be surprised if it was a simple case of drowning."

"I'm not so sure," Dr. McKenzie said. "He has a lot of bruising. Might be from the ice, but I can't say positively. Bad cut on his side too. Edges are so straight it makes me wonder. Won't know until an autopsy is done."

"You saying it was murder?" the constable asked.

"No, I'm just saying it's not obvious if he drowned or was dead before he went in the water." He turned to the detective. "How are we going to get him up to the road and onto the wagon?"

"Why not just roll him onto the blanket and carry him in it?" Barnes asked.

"Your skills at observation leave much to be desired," Hodgins replied. "The only thing holding that blanket together is the dirt and dust. Pick him up in it and he'd remain on the beach. What's that?" Hodgins pointed at the tarp that Ben had dropped beside the body.

"I grabbed the tarp when I got the blanket from the Yacht Club. Found it first, but I saw the blanket and figured it would be more respectful covering him with it rather than the tarp. Brought both back."

"It looks strong enough to hold the body," Hodgins said. We can each take a corner and carry him up to the buggy."

CHAPTER 2

Detective Albert Hodgins looked up as Dr. McKenzie approached his desk. "Well, Hamish, what can you tell me? Constable Barnes didn't take many notes at the scene yesterday." He held up the wrinkled receipt with a few lines of writing on the back. "I hope you have some information that will be of use." He let go of the receipt and watched it flutter down to the desk top, then gestured to the chair on the opposite side of his desk.

Dr. McKenzie sat down and placed a folder on the desk. "I'll write you out a copy of my notes in a few days, but I thought you'd want to hear what I found first."

McKenzie opened the folder, picked up the first sheet of paper, glanced at his notes, and relayed the information.

"I went through the pockets of the overcoat he was wearing. It had the name Lowe or Lorne stitched inside the collar. Not sure exactly as some of the stitches were gone. Didn't find much. He had sixty five cents and a train ticket, but the water has obliterated most of the printing.

He also had this key." He reached into his breast pocket, pulled out a tiny flat key, and handed it to Hodgins.

Hodgins had a quick look before placing it on his desk. "Looks like a trunk key."

McKenzie looked at his notes again. "He had on blue overalls, a smock, and felt lumberman boots." He looked up at Hodgins. "I thought he might be a farmer, but he doesn't have the weathered skin I'd expect of someone who works outside. Hands have calluses, and he is rather muscular, so I'd guess he does some sort of manual work, just not out in the sun all day."

He turned the page over and continued. "I'd estimate his age to be about twenty-five. Clean-shaven, about five foot eight and 160 pounds. Nothing wrong with his heart, liver or kidneys. He was in excellent health."

"I'll have someone check to see if we have a missing persons report matching that description. What about cause of death?"

"Well," Dr. McKenzie hesitated. "I didn't find any water in his lungs, and there was no foam around his mouth. I'd say he was dead before he hit the water."

"Are you suggesting foul play?"

McKenzie smiled. "That's for you to determine Detective. It's my job to tell you what I find, nothing more. There were a lot of marks on his body though."

"What type of marks?"

McKenzie put the page back in the folder and picked up another sheet. "Let's see. He had contusions everywhere. The one on the back of his head, just at the hair line, had the most peculiar shape. Something about it was familiar, but I just can't put my finger on it. I'm sure it will come to me though. He was also missing a lot of hair on the left side of his head, and the left side of his face, as you saw, was scraped clear down to the bone. That damage probably came from the ice, but some came from the gulls. He did have another interesting wound; I took a good look at that cut I pointed out to you at the scene - the one on his left side, just above his waist. It didn't look natural. Too straight and even to come from a fall or being pushed around in the water. It definitely came from a sharp, thin object. Probably a knife. The autopsy also showed that his skull was fractured. Split right through. No way the ice would have done that either. Had to have been something heavy and solid. Foul play or accident - well, you'll have to figure that out."

The coroner put the papers back in order and stood up. "I'll write up a copy for you as soon as I can." He picked up his folder and headed for the door whistling what Hodgins assumed was another of his old Scottish songs. It amazed him how the coroner always managed to be in such a jolly mood.

Hodgins had made notes while McKenzie spoke. He tore a clean sheet from his notebook and jotted down the physical description of the body. He looked around the station to see who was available.

"Barnes," he yelled. "Check this out." He held the paper and waited while Barnes made his way across the room, bumping into almost every desk along the way. "Description of the body from the harbour. Check missing persons."

Hodgins pushed Barnes' wrinkled receipt around the desk, then ran his hand over it in an attempt to flatten it. He opened his notebook and copied the few words written on the reverse. He cursed Barnes under his breath, and then started adding his own comments and questions.

Half an hour later Barnes was back. "I think I found him."

Hodgins raised one eyebrow.

Barnes, grinning from ear to ear, handed a missing persons report to the detective. "The description is almost an exact match, Sir."

Hodgins looked skeptical, but took the report and started to read it aloud. "Fred Walker, age twenty six, 162 pounds, five foot seven. Age, weight and height seem to fit, but the name on the coat was Lorne or Lowe, not

Walker."

"Keep reading, Sir."

Hodgins glared at Barnes, and the grin quickly disappeared from the young constable's face. "Sir," he stammered. "Look at the name of the person who filed the report."

Hodgins looked down at the report. "Well, Barnes. I do believe you have redeemed yourself - somewhat." Without looking up, he waved a hand at Barnes, indicating he was dismissed.

Barnes backed away and stumbled over a chair. "Thank you, Sir." He turned and raced back to his desk.

Hodgins looked up, shook his head and mumbled, "Clumsy git." He looked back at the missing persons report and re-read the name. George Lowe, Stouffville, cousin of Fred Walker. "Barnes," he bellowed. "Fetch me a train schedule."

* * *

Hodgins hopped off the trolley at the end of his road, and walked to the house he shared with his wife's family. He enjoyed living in the upscale neighbourhood, but wished he could afford a little house of his own. He opened the front door and his eight year old daughter, Sara, ran into his arms. He was astounded how she could greet him with such gusto day after day, as though he'd been away for months, not hours.

She helped him off with his coat and hung it on the lower hook of the coat tree. "Can we go skating tonight Daddy? Please?"

Sara had received a new pair of skates for Christmas and wanted to use them every day.

He took her hand and followed the aroma of the meal down the hall and into the kitchen. "Not tonight. You'll have to wait until Saturday."

Sara pouted, her lower lip quivering. "Just for a little while?"

He looked down at her sad face and smiled. "The skating rink won't be open after supper, and the ice on the pond isn't thick enough. We'll make a day of it on Saturday. Skating in the morning, then we'll have lunch somewhere – you pick. Then we can go to the display at the Crystal Palace. Just you, me and Mother. How does that sound?"

Sara's face lit up. "Skating and the Crystal Palace? Really Daddy? Oh yes, please."

In the kitchen Hodgins' wife, Cordelia, and her mother, were putting the finishing touches on dinner. Physically, his wife was a younger version of Euphemia. Both had wavy orange-ish-red hair. Their completions were fair, but unlike her mother Cordelia had a smattering of freckles across her cheeks and nose. They had the same green eyes, but Hodgins could see Cordelia's held a sparkle that was missing from his mother-in-law's. He kissed his wife on the cheek, then nodded at Euphemia, but said nothing to her.

"Irish stew. Smells wonderful, as usual," he said.

"Have you found out who that unfortunate man from the harbour is?"

"Possibly. We have a lead that I'll be checking out tomorrow. Have to take the train to Stouffville first thing in the morning."

"Was he murdered?"

"Really Cordelia," her mother exclaimed. "Why would you want to know such a thing?"

Cordelia enjoyed listening to her husband talk about his cases. At first, Hodgins felt the same as his mother-in-law. Women, proper ladies, should find murder morbid, frightening, something not to be discussed. However, he quickly discovered that by talking to Cordelia she helped him sort out his thoughts with her sharp, logical mind. More than once she noticed some minor detail that he had dismissed as unimportant, and he was able to link it to one or more other clues that helped him solve a case. He soon realized that going over the details with her helped him put everything in order. Hodgins looked forward to their evening chats. He picked up a spoon and sampled the stew.

"Tastes even better than it smells." He dropped the spoon in the sink and made his way to the front parlour to sit with his father-in-law Harold, and wait to be called to the table.

CHAPTER 3

Hodgins exited the train and stood on the platform at the Stouffville station buttoning up his overcoat. The platform filled with people going about their business; several business men heading to Toronto, a few salesmen with their sample cases, ladies heading out for a day of shopping he figured, and families off somewhere on a trip. The hiss of the breaks startled him. He watched as steam billowed out the entire length of the train, causing one lady's dress to swirl around her legs when she walked too close. A gust of wind blew the steam back under the train and caused Hodgins to duck when a derby hat shot past his head. Looking around for the ticket booth, he spotted one a few feet away, just outside the station house.

He walked over and asked the ticket man, "Can you direct me to Second Street?"

"Of course, Sir. It's not far." He pointed towards the south end of the platform. "Just go to Main Street there and turn right. First street you come to is Edward. Turn right again and the next street is Second."

Hodgins was glad the house wasn't far. He nodded his thanks and began walking, raising his collar to try to block the stinging wind. There wasn't much snow on the ground, so he knew at least his feet would be reasonably warm, despite the thinning soles on his patent leather boots.

He stopped briefly along the way to admire an enormous brick house, complete with gingerbread and a turret. It was just the type of house Cordelia would love to own. He couldn't wait for the day he, Cordelia, and Sara could move into a place of their own. He imagined Cordelia in the springtime, standing on the second floor balcony watching ladies strolling with their baby carriages, enjoying the sounds of the returning robins, and the scents of the flowering crab apple trees. Too bad this house was so close to the noisy train station. He wouldn't want to listen to the steam whistle and hissing breaks every day. With one last wishful look, he continued along Second, looking for the Lowe home.

A few minutes later Hodgins climbed the steps of a covered, white-washed porch attached to a little brick house at the corner of Second and Williams. He took a quick peek in the window as he crossed to the door. Fortunately there was no one in the room to see him snoop. The little wrought iron bench at the far corner of the porch looked inviting, despite the weather. He could picture himself sitting there in the summer early in the morning, watching the neighbours and enjoying a warm breeze.

He reached for the door knocker and noticed it wasn't the usual type. Instead of a hoop or straight knocker, this one was shaped like a hand holding a ball. *Silly thing to waste money on*, he thought. Hodgins lifted the hand and rapped it against the door three times then turned around and took in the surroundings. Except for the noise coming from the train station, it was very quiet. The soft whinny of a horse touched his ears, but he wasn't able to tell where it came from. The street was a mixture of large and small homes; some yellow brick, others red, with baton homes scattered throughout. Both sides of the street were lined with Maple and Oak trees. *Probably cool in the summer under the canopy of all those trees*, he thought, unlike the street he lived on. This would be a nice place to raise a family. Too bad it wasn't close to his police station.

Hodgins heard someone moving inside and turned back just as the door opened. A pleasant looking woman, wearing a dark blue dress and a flour covered apron, greeted him. Hodgins guessed she was his wife's age - early-thirties. He held up his badge and introduced himself.

"I'm looking for Mr. Lowe. Is he home?"

"Please, come in. I'm Mrs. Lowe." She turned and called for her husband. A slightly balding man, closer to forty, came downstairs and stood beside his wife.

"I'm George Lowe. What can I do for you?"

"You filed a missing persons report on your cousin, Fred Walker. Is there someplace we can talk?"

"Oh, where are my manners," Mrs. Lowe said. "Come in to the drawing room." She moved down the hall and opened a door. "Would you like some tea to take the chill away?"

"That would be nice, thank you," Hodgins said. Mrs. Lowe went to prepare the tea and George gestured for Hodgins to enter the parlour. He walked in, and went straight over to the fire to warm himself. George followed, closing the door behind him.

"Detective, where's Fred? Have you located him?"

"I'm afraid the news is not good. A body was found on a beach in Toronto. He fits the general description of your cousin." Hodgins pulled his notebook and pencil out of his coat pocket.

"We're not positive that he is your cousin. I don't want to go into too much detail, but it is difficult to identify him. The coroner has called an inquest for Wednesday at the Queen's Hotel in Toronto. We'll need

21

you to come in and identify the body beforehand. If it is Fred, you'll have to attend the inquest."

George stared at the detective for a moment. "What do you mean it's difficult to identify him?"

"He was in the water and his face was damaged, quite possibly by the ice in the harbour. We haven't determined what caused the other wounds. The overcoat he was wearing had your name stitched into the collar."

George grabbed the back of the nearest chair. "Yes, it's possible. Fred borrowed it from time to time."

"I'm sorry to bring you such bad news, and so early in the morning, but I wanted to catch you before you left for work." Without waiting for an invitation, Hodgins sat on the matching chair opposite George. He noticed that the padded tapestry on the arms was a little thin and faded. He crossed his right leg, the ankle resting on his left knee, and used his inner thigh as a table for his notebook. The sun shone through the side window, illuminating the pages and pulling some of the winter chill from his face.

"Are you aware of any problems Fred had lately? Any arguments? Someone who may have had a grudge against him for any reason?"

"No," George said. He thought for a moment, chewing his lower lip. "Well . . ."

Hodgins perched his pencil over the notebook,

waiting.

George continued, "He was quite upset on Christmas day. I'm sure it's not connected."

"I'll be the judge of that. Something you consider trivial could be very important. What was he upset about?"

"A woman."

"Ah," Hodgins said. "You'd better start at the beginning."

George sighed and slumped down onto the chair.

"It started years ago, back in England. We hail from Norfolk. Fred was very close to a girl named Emily. After Fred's mother died, his father remarried. His new wife didn't get along with his children, so they were sent here to live with their aunt, my mother. Fred spoke of Emily often."

George sat up straight and put one hand over his mouth, then dragged it down over his beard. "Dear Lord. His brother and sister. They'll have to be told. Neither lives in town. Henry is a farmhand a few miles north, and Anabelle just married this past summer before moving to Schomberg."

George paused while Hodgins wrote everything down.

Hodgins look up and said, "Continue please."

"Two years ago, Emily's family moved here. Actually,

they only live a few blocks away on Albert Street. They became friendly again. On Christmas morning, around 10:30 I believe, Fred walked to her house for a visit. I recall the time because my wife had just put the bird in the oven. Said it needed exactly six hours, and we planned Christmas dinner for 4:30. He was back home before noon, and very agitated."

Hodgins wrote for a few moments. "Did he say why he was upset?"

George stood and walked to the fireplace. He picked up a pipe from the mantle, reached into his pocket for his tobacco pouch and filled the bowl. He lit it and turned back to the detective.

"He wouldn't talk about it at first, and we didn't want to pry. At dinner he just blurted it out. Apparently, when he arrived at the Smythe's he discovered Emily had married a few days earlier. We knew she had other gentlemen callers, but we all assumed she would eventually marry Fred. He was just promoted to foreman at the sawmill and was planning to propose after the new year. We were all shocked."

Hodgins thought for a moment, wrote in his book, and then said, "Interesting. Did Fred speak to Emily after that?"

George shrugged. "I don't know. Fred didn't mention

her again. He kept to himself the next several days. Then, on the twenty-ninth, he was out of sorts all day. Distracted. After supper he went up to his room and we didn't see him again. Neither of us heard anything from him; didn't notice him go out. We just assumed he was in his room all night. My wife called him for breakfast but he didn't come down. She went up to his room, and he wasn't there. He must have risen early. I suppose he could have snuck out any time really."

"I'll need the full name and address of Emily."

"Emily lived with her parents, the Smythe's, at number five Albert Street. Afraid I don't know who she married, or where they live. Fred never said."

The door opened and Mrs. Lowe came in carrying a tray with a pot of tea, milk, sugar, and cups. The aroma of baking bread wafted into the room and Hodgins took a deep, satisfying breath. It was one of his favourite scents. She placed the tray on a small table beside the sofa and started to pour. Hodgins noticed she brought three cups and was still wearing the flour covered apron.

"Grace, this conversation is not something you need to hear," Mr. Lowe said.

She ignored him and handed Hodgins the first cup of tea. "Milk and sugar?" she asked.

"Thank you, no, black is fine. We were just discussing

25

Miss Smythe's marriage. Don't suppose you know who she married?"

Mrs. Lowe poured some tea for her husband and a cup for herself, then made herself comfortable on the sofa, despite the scowl from George. "No, and it's the strangest thing. There was no announcement in church. I wondered why the Smythes didn't attend the service Christmas Eve. I was just saying to Louise, our neighbour, how odd it was that Emily was married without a big wedding. Well, there's usually only one reason why someone gets wed quickly without any fuss."

"Grace," George said. "You know how I feel about gossip. You'll have to excuse my wife, Detective. She does like to talk."

Hodgins made more notes, then closed the notebook and slipped it into his coat pocket with the pencil stub. "Quite all right." He turned to Mrs. Lowe and smiled. "I completely understand what you mean, Madame." He blew on his hot tea, took a sip, then turned his attention back to Mr. Lowe.

"I have a few more calls to make, but I need to ask one more thing. Did Fred have a trunk?"

"Yes. He brought one with him when he moved in with us last year after my mother passed," George said. "Why?"

"We found a key in his pocket. I'd like to see if it fits his trunk." He took one large gulp of his tea then reached over and put his cup on the tray.

George pointed up. "It's in his room, upstairs."

Hodgins stood and waited for Mr. Lowe to show him the way. "Sir?"

George looked up at the detective, not sure what to do.

"The trunk?"

"Sorry, I was just thinking about poor Fred. It's this way."

"Poor Fred?" Mrs. Lowe asked. "George, what is going on?"

"They may have found him. I'll tell you later." He got up, put his cup and saucer on the tray.

Grace turned to Hodgins. "What happened to Fred? What aren't you telling me?"

"I said I'd tell you later," George said. "Just wait here until the detective leaves."

He led Hodgins to Fred's room at the end of the hall on the second floor.

Hodgins asked George where the trunk was kept. George shrugged. "Never really noticed."

Hodgins stood just inside the door and looked around the small bedroom; bed by the window, wash stand beside the bed, dresser against the wall beside the door, small table and chair against the far wall. There was no trunk in sight. There was a door in the wall opposite the table that Hodgins assumed was a closet. He walked over and opened the door. The trunk was against the back wall. He dragged it out, and then took the key out of his shirt pocket.

George came closer to watch as Hodgins opened the trunk. There was a barely audible click as he turned the key. Hodgins lifted the lid and both men looked in. Hodgins pulled out a couple of old grey work shirts, just like the one that the dead man wore, and a photo.

"Blast. I thought there would be something in here," Hodgins said. He dropped the shirts back into the trunk and turned the picture so George could look at it.

"That's Fred," George said.

Hodgins looked up. "I'll need to take this photo with me." Are you able to come to the coroner's office Monday? We have to find out if the body really is your cousin." George nodded.

They went back downstairs and Hodgins thanked the Lowe's for their time. Hodgins put his collar up as he went out into the cold again. Following the directions George had given him, he was at the Smythe home in no time. Another red brick house. Hodgins was amazed at both the differences and similarities between this small town and Toronto. In the city, there were rows of houses all the same, making it easy to go to the wrong door if you weren't paying attention. Here, the houses were of a different design, but again, many were almost identical. In the dark it would be very easy to walk into someone else's home by mistake.

Hodgins knocked on the front door three times before anyone answered. The door jerked open, and a stout, annoyed, older gentleman stared at Hodgins.

"Yes, what do you want?" he barked.

Once again, Hodgins showed his badge. "I have some questions about Mr. Walker." The man introduced himself as Mr. Smythe and lead Hodgins into the front room.

"Yes, Fred Walker was here Christmas day. Came to call on my daughter. Why are the police interested in that?"

"Mr. Walker is missing. I need to speak with everyone who was here that day. I understand your daughter is recently married. Where might I find her?"

Mr. Smythe hesitated for a moment, then revealed that Emily and her new husband were living with the Smythes temporarily and went to fetch them. Hodgins walked over to the fireplace to warm himself. He looked around the room, noticing the difference between this home and the Lowe's. A large painting of Queen Victoria hung over the mantle with a small British flag sitting on either side. The floral wallpaper looked new, the colours still vibrant. He walked around the room examining the carvings on the furniture's walnut arms, running his hand along the grain, and admiring the high quality of the workmanship. While not rich, the Smythes seemed quite comfortable in their circumstances. He turned when he heard the door open.

A young woman in her early twenties, who he assumed to be Emily, entered followed by her father and a rather plain but well dressed man. He could see why more than one man would be interested in Emily. Though not what most people would consider beautiful, she was one of the most striking women he had ever seen. Despite the bustle protruding at the back, and the numerous layers of fabric, he could tell she had an excellent figure, and there was something about those large, green eyes. Hodgins realized he was staring, and turned his attention back to Mr. Smythe.

Mr. Smythe introduced his daughter and her husband, Patrick Flanagan, who looked like he wasn't that much younger than Emily's father. She certainly had not married the better looking of her two suitors, judging by the picture of Fred he had in his breast pocket.

"My father-in-law said you wished to speak to us about the disappearance of Mr. Walker," Mr. Flanagan said.

Emily perched on the edge of the chair closest to the fire, and Patrick joined Hodgins in front of the fireplace. Hodgins took the notebook and stubby pencil out of his coat pocket and flipped through the pages, careful not to tear them.

"Most disagreeable chap, Walker," Patrick said. "Works at my mill. A common labourer."

Hodgins looked over at Emily and could see the deep concern on her face. He'd seen that look dozens of times over his career with the police. She was still in love with Walker.

"I believe Mr. Walker came here on Christmas Day?"

"Yes, that's correct," Patrick said. "Took the wind out of his sails when I told him Emily had married me only days earlier." A nasty little grin crept across Patrick's face. "He said some rather unpleasant things, and I practically had to throw him out the door. I may have shoved him off the porch to hurry him along. Haven't seen him since. Gone off to lick his wounds, I suppose."

Hodgins wrote a few words in his notebook, and then addressed Emily. "Have you seen Mr. Walker since Christmas, Mrs. Flanagan?"

Emily shook her head. "No," she said quietly. "Do you have any idea where he is?"

Hodgins hesitated, trying to decide how much he should reveal. "We found a man that fits his general description. George Lowe will be coming to Toronto to positively identify the body on Monday."

Emily's mouth formed a perfect tiny 'O', but no sound came out. She looked at her husband, then fell back in the chair. Her eyelids fluttered, and Hodgins thought she was about to faint. Rather than being alarmed, Patrick seemed put out by his wife's reaction. Sighing, he walked to the door, opened it, and called for Emily's mother to bring the salts.

Hodgins heard footsteps running down the hall and a plump, cheery looking woman hurried through the doorway carrying two small bottles: one containing crystals, the other was labeled ammonia. She placed the bottles on a small end table and opened them. She was just about to pour the ammonia over the crystals when Emily spoke.

"Put those away, Mother. I'm perfectly fine. I just had a bad shock. The detective told us that Freddie is dead." She pulled a lacy handkerchief out of her dress sleeve and dabbed her eyes. "It's dreadful." She raised the kerchief and covered her face.

"Freddie? You mean Fred Walker?" Mrs. Smythe asked her daughter. She stood beside the chair and cradled Emily's head against her chest.

"You'll have to leave now," Patrick said. "This has all been too much for my wife."

"Too much?" Emily got up from the chair. "Fred was a childhood friend. How do you expect me to react?"

Mrs. Smythe took her daughter's hand and led her out of the room. Hodgins could hear Emily sobbing as her mother took her upstairs.

Hodgins made a few more notes, checked his pocket watch, and then left. It wasn't quite noon yet, but he decided to have an early meal and a nice, hot cup of tea at the tavern beside the train station. It would be a more pleasant meal than whatever they had available on the train, and he could sit and enjoy it without rocking back and forth. *Might actually get to finish the tea this time*, he thought.

Despite it only being 11:30 a.m., the tavern had a lot of patrons, and he enjoyed listening to the sounds of murmuring voices, and the clinking of glasses and cutlery. The large windows at the front and side of the tavern allowed in sufficient light so none of the lanterns were currently lit. The pub near his station house had tiny windows and the lanterns were lit at all times. While he loved his wife's Irish cooking, he longed for some traditional English food. His mouth watered at the thought of Cottage Pie, a standard at most pubs. He loved the minced meat, mixed with peas and carrots, topped with mashed potatoes smothered in gravy. Hodgins hoped they served it in this little town.

He sat at a table near the oak bar and asked the bartender what was good. As soon as he heard Cottage Pie he knew what he was ordering. When it came, he took his time eating, savouring every bite. Just as he finished his Darjeeling tea, the tall clock in the corner chimed, reminding him he had to return to Toronto. He bundled up, and made his way back to the station.

* * *

The train started to move as soon as he sat down. When the conductor came by to punch his ticket, it reminded him of the washed out one that had been found in Fred's overcoat. He pulled the picture of Fred out of his pocket.

"Ever seen this guy?" he asked the conductor.

"Yes, Sir. That's young Fred. Works at the mill with my boy. Hasn't been around for a while though."

"When did you see him last?"

"Hmm, let me think." The conductor scratched the side of his neck a few times and looked up at the roof of the train car. "I believe it was on the train. Yes, I'm sure of it. I remember the argument."

"When? Who was he arguing with?"

"Just after Christmas. Not more than three or four days later, I'm sure of that."

"The argument, who was it with? Did you hear what they fought about?"

"Well, wasn't really a proper argument. Fred was very agitated. Funny thing. Mr. Flanagan was laughing. Couldn't hear what it was about. Not my place to listen in on private conversations anyway."

"Flanagan? Patrick Flanagan?"

The conductor wrinkled his nose. "Yes, that's him. I think that's the first time I ever heard him laugh. Can't tell you no more. That's all I saw."

"Thank you. You've been most helpful."

The conductor nodded and moved to the next seat to continue punching tickets, leaving Hodgins to wonder what had transpired between the two men. Mr. Walker was apparently angry, yet Flanagan laughed. *Could he have been taunting Fred? Why were they on the train together?*

CHAPTER 4

All through breakfast Sara chatted to her grandparents about her plans for the day; ice skating uppermost in her mind.

"It will be so much fun," Sara said. "I haven't been skating for such a long time."

"You know that's not true," Cordelia said. "Just a few days ago you were skating with your friend Laura."

"But that was just a tiny ice surface her father made in the back yard."

Hodgins laughed and turned to his wife. "My dear, skating on a ice surface someone's father made just doesn't count. It's not really skating unless you are on a pond or creek, or even the city rink."

"Oh how silly of me to forget." Cordelia looked across the table at Sara and smiled. "I do apologize. You were correct. You haven't skated in weeks."

Everyone burst out laughing, even the normally dour Euphemia. Sara just sat looking puzzled.

Once breakfast was over, Cordelia, her mother, and Sara, started clearing the table and doing the washing up. Harold disappeared to the back of the house, and Hodgins went into the front room to read the early edition of the Daily Globe. He pulled a chair near the fireplace and sat with his legs stretched towards the crackling fire.

He could hear Sara asking about the Crystal Palace and had a quick look the at paper to see if there was any mention of the current exhibit. There was nothing. He hoped it would be something of interest to a little girl. On page three he noticed an advertisement for houses and building lots for sale. The house on Elm Street was of interest; brick, ten rooms and bathroom, gas, and grates. He carefully tore it out and placed it in his vest pocket.

The sounds of clinking china and cutlery died down, so Hodgins got up and went back into the kitchen. Sara was sweeping the floor and Cordelia was cleaning the counter while Euphemia wiped the table. Since the cleanup was done, Hodgins announced it was time to go. Cordelia went upstairs to change her clothes and Sara raced to the front door. She removed her bright green cape with the rabbit fur collar from the hook and wrapped herself up. Picking up the skate blades that were waiting by the door, she was ready to go before Hodgins finished speaking.

"Sara, don't run through the house like that," her

grandmother scolded. "You're a lady, not a ruffian."

"Leave her be," Hodgins said. "She's excited. I don't often have a free Saturday, and she's been looking forward to spending time with her mother and me for days." He turned and smiled at his daughter. "She'll be lady-like."

Sara nodded her head eagerly. "Oh, yes, Daddy. I'll be good. Can we go now?"

Euphemia said, "You spoil that child." She made a face and went upstairs, passing Cordelia on her way down.

"Why does your mother always look like she's just eaten a lemon?"

"Oh, Bertie. Why can't you just get along with Mother?"

"I've tried. Lord knows I've tried. She never got over the fact I didn't complete my schooling. She'd rather her daughter married a respectable lawyer, and not," he winked, "a lowly man of the law."

"Albert Hodgins, are you trying to flirt with me?" Cordelia laughed softly and touched his cheek. "You don't do that often enough."

Cordelia's father came down the hallway carrying two sets of skate blades so Hodgins and Cordelia could skate with Sara and not just watch. "Found them. I knew I'd seen them on the back porch. Someone had thrown an old towel over them." He handed Hodgins the skate blades and said, "You're right. She does look like she's eaten a lemon."

"Daddy," Sara whined from the front door.

"Off with you now. I don't think that child will last a moment longer," Harold said.

Hodgins, Cordelia, and Sara walked to the corner to catch the trolley down to Gerrard Street, where they changed to another that took them to the skating rink on Sherbourne. Sara sat at the back, waving to everyone she saw.

The trolley stopped in front of the rink. They couldn't see the ice through the high wooden fence that surrounded it, but could hear voices and laughter as they walked to the entrance. Hodgins was surprised at the large number of people already there. It was a nice day and it looked like half the city was enjoying it.

While he was strapping the skate blades to Sara's boots, one of her friends came over. She couldn't wait to tell Sara all about the new puppy she got. Sara squealed with delight. "A puppy!" She turned to her parents. "May I go over and see it today?"

Cordelia nodded, "I'll take you over before supper."

Sara grabbed her friend's hand and skated off.

Hodgins' knelt in front of the bench and fastened a pair of blades to his wife's boots, then sat beside her and put on his own. "I wish we could do this more often. We don't spend nearly enough time together. Maybe this summer I can get some time off and we can rent a cottage somewhere."

Cordelia looked at him, surprised. "Do you mean that Bertie? We haven't been on a proper holiday since before Sara was born."

"Can't promise anything, but I'll try. I'll ask the criminals to take a few weeks off." He waved at Sara as she skated past with her friend.

"It would be nice to have a dog," he said. "We could take it on long walks, and it would teach Sara responsibility too."

"You know mother can't abide animals in the house."

He stood and held his hand out to Cordelia. "I know," he said with a grin.

* * *

Hodgins stomped his feet, removing most of the slush from his boots before entering the house. He dropped the skate blades just inside the door, hung his overcoat on the coat tree and walked into the front room. His father-in-law, Harold Campbell, was snoozing in the overstuffed chair that Harold had declared to be 'his' chair. He woke at the sound of Hodgins pouring a glass of whiskey.

"Don't mind if I do," he said.

Hodgins poured a second glass and handed it to Harold on his way to the settee. He downed his drink in one gulp, set the glass on the carpet, then stretched out - feet hanging over the far arm of the settee.

"Oh, my poor feet. I could walk all day, but skating for an hour is too much. My ankles weren't made for balancing on thin blades."

"I remember days skating with Euphemia and Cordelia," Harold said. "They both enjoyed it so much. Didn't really care for it myself, but it was pleasant to sit and watch them. I wish I could have gone with you, but my leg won't let me." He rubbed his right leg for a moment. "Damn weather. Cold makes it ache more. A sport best left for the young. Speaking of which, what did you do with my grand-daughter? I don't hear her or Cordelia."

"They went to Sara's friend's house - that girl with the fizzy brown hair. Never could remember her name. She was at the rink and told Sara about her new puppy, so Sara had to see it." Hodgins got up, scooped his empty glass off the carpet, and went over to the tantalus on the sideboard to pour another whiskey.

"Can't picture Euphemia skating. Can't image her doing anything fun, no offense."

"None taken," Harold laughed. "She was different

41

when she was younger. After my accident, we didn't get out much."

A sharp knock on the door interrupted their conversation. Hodgins got up. "Now what?" He looked out the front window. "It's Barnes, one of my constables. Guess my day off is over."

Hodgins answered the door and let the young constable in.

"Sorry to disturb you, Sir, but I was told to fetch you right away. Something about the bloke they found in the harbour."

Hodgins sighed, and put on his coat. "Let's go."

They walked to the corner and waited for the trolley. Barnes stared at his feet, avoiding eye contact. Hodgins noticed the man's discomfort.

"Don't fret lad. It's not the first time I've been called from my day off. It certainly won't be the last."

Hodgins tried to have a conversation with the constable, but only received one or two word answers, so he gave up and they rode to the station in silence.

Hodgins walked through the station house to his desk, and saw a man and boy seated in front of it. He recognized the gentleman immediately - Ben Grove. "What can I do for you, Mr. Grove?"

"This is my youngest lad, Danny. He has something

that may be of interest to you."

Hodgins extended his hand. "Nice to meet you Danny. What do you have?"

Danny shook the detective's hand briefly, then snatched it back as though afraid. Hodgins walked around his desk and sat down. He looked from Danny to Mr. Grove.

"Well?"

Mr. Grove tapped Danny lightly on the knee. "Show him."

Danny stood up, reached into his pants pocket and pulled something out. He kept his hand clenched and looked at his father. Ben nodded toward Hodgins. Danny extended his arm and opened his fist.

Hodgins reached out and took the round, white object. "Looks like a pearl cufflink."

"Says it was lying beside the body." Ben said. "Grabbed it before his bother pulled him away. My wife found it in their room this morning. Soon as he told where he got it, I knew we had to turn it over."

"Thank you for bring it in," Hodgins said to Danny. "It was the right thing to do."

As Ben and Danny left the station, Danny glanced back at the detective and smiled.

Hodgins turned the cufflink over in his hands,

wondering what connection it had with the body, if any. *Expensive looking.* He got up and walked over to a window. It glistened in the sunlight. He was certain it was a real pearl and just as sure that Mr. Walker could not afford such luxury.

CHAPTER 5

Monday morning George Lowe arrived in Toronto to view the body that had been pulled out of Toronto Harbour five days earlier. Hodgins led him to the morgue. Dr. McKenzie had the body laid out on a steel table, with a clean, white sheet covering him. George slowly moved beside the table and looked down at the shape. He took two deep breaths and nodded once. Dr. McKenzie lifted the sheet so only the right side of his face was visible. George gasped and took a step back. "It's Fred."

Hodgins waited several minutes as George composed himself. "I'm sorry for your loss. I realize this has been hard and you need to go home and start making arrangements, but I have to ask you a few more questions.

George nodded. "When can I bring him home for burial? We need to set up the front parlour and prepare his body for visitations."

"Probably in a few days," Hodgins said. "Do you

recall if your cousin mentioned a fight with Emily's husband?"

"No, not that I can recall. Now that you mention it though, his trousers were rather dirty and wet when he came home Christmas day. His clothes were spotless when he went out. My wife commented on it, but I didn't give it a second thought. And he was rubbing his leg a bit. Was there an altercation at the Smythe's?"

"Mr. Flanagan said he threw Fred out."

"Flanagan? Patrick Flanagan? That's who she wed? I can't believe Emily married that bully. No wonder Fred was in such a state. Her parents probably had a hand in that. That would explain why it was kept quiet. I can't think of anyone who would have attended. Patrick Flanagan is not a popular man."

"Why is that? Because of his business dealings? Or maybe his personality? What would stop the neighbours from attending a rich man's wedding?"

Lowe twisted his wedding ring. I don't like to speak ill of people."

"Your cousin is dead. Don't you want to find out what happened? It's your duty to tell me everything you know."

Lowe let out a soft sigh. "It's a bit of both, but mostly business. Flanagan was feared by anyone who had dealings with him. But he does have money. The Smythe's would probably overlook everything else if they could marry Emily to someone well off."

Hodgins raised an eyebrow. "Was he violent or just hard and unfeeling?"

"He certainly was unfeeling, but he was never physically violent. Not as far as I know. He would on occasion be overheard threatening someone. A day or two later that person would have cuts or bruises. Sometimes worse. Flanagan was always someplace public when it happened. I've heard rumours that he pays someone to rough up anyone who doesn't cooperate, but it's only rumour."

"How does he make his money?"

"He's a businessman," Lowe replied. "He owns the mill where Fred worked. Also owns several properties that he rents out. Business as well as a few small homes. Even has some low rent properties in Toronto. I believe he travels there regularly to collect the rent personally."

Hodgins mulled that over. "If he's so well off, why is he living with the Smythe's? Doesn't he have his own house?"

"Yes, he has a large home on Victoria Street. I've noticed workmen there a lot lately. Probably staying with the Smythe's until the work is done. Oh, I remembered something after you left. In November, Fred was promoted to foreman at the mill. One of the other workers was expecting to get the position and accused Fred of buying the job. There was a fight. Fred was beat up pretty bad."

Hodgins picked up his pencil and flipped open his notebook. "I'll need this man's name."

"Fred never said who it was."

Hodgins closed his notebook. "Appreciate your help Mr. Lowe. I'll see what I can find out. Someone will contact you when you can come to collect your cousin's body."

George Lowe stood up and reached across the desk to shake the detective's hand.

Mr. Lowe left, and Hodgins picked up the folder containing the coroner's report. He had lost count of how many times he read, and re-read the contents. He opened his notebook again and studied the notes he took while at the Lowe's home. Everything seemed to revolve around Emily and her marriage to a wealthy, and apparently nasty, man. Where were these low rent properties in Toronto? Were they even relevant?

Hodgins grabbed his coat and hat and went outside to wait for the horse-drawn trolley to take him up to the Records Office to find the properties that Flanagan owned. Over the next few hours Hodgins sat hunched over a small table making pages of notes. He was completely unaware of the time until one of the clerks tapped him on the shoulder and pointed to his pocket watch.

Hodgins gathered up his papers and decided to walk back to the station. Along the way he stopped at a street vendor and purchased a pork pie. When he got back to the station house, he went around to the side, looking for the stray mutt. He spotted it curled up in the crate that had been put out by one of the men. He dropped a few pieces of pie in the crate, and went in the side door.

CHAPTER 6

Hodgins paced around the station waiting for Barnes, his head whipping around every time the door opened. The young constable finally entered the station house and Hodgins raced to his side. He whisked Barnes back out giving him a little nudge to hurry him along, causing the constable to stumble on the steps. Hodgins grabbed his arm and mumbled an apology, but didn't slow down.

"Where we off to Sir, if you don't mind me asking?"

"Train," Hodgins said as he rushed ahead. The street was filling with vendors and storekeepers, anxious to start the day. Barnes trotted along dodging the newsboys, trying to keep up with the detective's long strides.

By the time they arrived at Union Station Barnes was out of breath. Hodgins shook his head.

"You need to exercise more lad. Only a few blocks and you can hardly breathe. You should join the YMCA. They opened up one a few blocks from the station. Do you a world of good."

Before Barnes could think of a reply Hodgins was halfway to the ticket booth, leaving the constable standing by the door. He was back a few minutes later with two return tickets to Stouffville and a schedule.

"Train leaves in twenty-five minutes. There's an empty bench over there."

They sat in silence for about five minutes before Barnes worked up the courage to ask, "Who are we going to see?"

"I need to talk to the men at the mill. Find out who started the fight."

"Fight, Sir?"

"Seems one of the men was less than pleased that Mr. Walker was promoted. Have to find out who it was." Hodgins pulled his notebook out of his pocket, turned to the last page of writing and read the notes he made after Lowe had identified the body. "Back in November. Maybe the fight was about more than a lost promotion." He closed the small book and slipped it back into his pocket. He turned to face Barnes. "You need to ask around about Mrs. Flanagan. See if anyone knows why she married that arrogant man. Find out who her friends are. They may know something. You're about the same age - might be more apt to tell you things."

Barnes nodded in agreement as a conductor called for passengers to board. Hurrying to the train, Hodgins patted his overcoat pocket.

"Barnes, don't suppose you have a notebook?"

The constable smiled and reached into his pocket. He proudly pulled out a small, shiny leather-bound notebook.

"Got one last evening. Sir. I noticed you carry yours all the time and I figured I should have one too." He put his hand back into his pocket and drew out not one, but two pencils, freshly sharpened. He held them out for the detective's inspection.

Hodgins glanced at Barnes' purchases. "You're a quick learner Barnes. You just might make Sergeant some day."

* * *

The ride to Stouffville was uneventful and quiet. Hodgins read his note over and over. He jotted down questions, and underlined or circled items to follow up on.

Barnes chatted to a salesman who boarded at Riverdale and exited at Milliken. He watched Hodgins work away at his notes until they arrived at Unionville. An elderly lady who was travelling alone boarded. She reminded Barnes of his grandmother. He got up and sat with her for the rest of his ride.

By the time the train pulled into the Stouffville

station, the sun was shining. It was still a bit nippy, but there was little wind and the sky was almost void of clouds. Hodgins commented how different it was from the previous Saturday.

"Hardly a soul around. Suppose Tuesday is not a busy day. Guess most people are already at work, like that gent over there." He pointed at a rail employee who was sweeping the last of the snow off the platform.

As they left the train station in Stouffville Hodgins pointed west. "The Smythes and Lowes live over there." Stopping at the end of the platform Hodgins turned east.

"There's the top of the mill. I believe there are a few shops a little further along. I'll see what I can find out from the mill workers and you talk to everyone you can. There must be plenty of folks in the shops who know Mrs. Flanagan. Find out if there's any gossip. It's a small town and people tend to talk. We'll meet up at the tavern beside the station for lunch."

They crossed a side rail and passed a large building on the opposite side of the road. Barnes pinched his nose. "Don't need to read the sign to know that's a tannery. How do those poor buggers stand it day after day?"

"Don't suppose they have much choice," Hodgins replied. Barnes stepped off the plank sidewalk to cross a narrow lane. Hodgins reached out and pulled him back. A wagon loaded with logs came thundering down. The pair of black draft horses stopped at the cross-road. The wheels of the wagon sent a spray of slush up onto the plank walkway, just missing Hodgins and Barnes. The horses snorted and stomped their large, hair-covered feet.

A farmer was coming across the main road at the same time. His horse reared up. They met the draft horses at the corner. The farmer flicked his reins and the chestnut nag settled down and trotted along. The man with the load of logs seemed to be looking for something in his pocket, paying little or no attention to his surroundings.

Barnes drew in a breath. "That was close. Good thing you yanked me out of the way. I could have been trampled. And I though for sure the logging wagon was going to plow right into that farmer."

Hodgins shrugged. "Imagine the beasts have been up and down that road so many times, they know what to do. Smart creatures, horses are. Smarter than a lot of folk I know."

The horses started moving again, crossing the road to the mill. "I'll follow this chap, and you see if you can find someone to open up about the Flanagans. And try to remember we are investigating a possible murder. This is not a social call."

"Sir?"

"I noticed you chatting it up with the salesman and lady on the train. You can be very talkative. Let the people here have a chance to speak."

Barnes' ears turned red, and he stood looking like a scolded puppy.

"I'm not saying it's bad to be social, just keep in mind why we're here. You're good with people. Use it."

Barnes smiled. "Thank you, Sir. I'll try to talk less."

Hodgins nodded and crossed the muddy road heading towards the mill. The sounds of saws and rattling chains increased with each step. The pair of draft horses stood by a set of large doors waiting while the logs were unstrapped.

"Who's in charge here?" Hodgins asked.

"Don't need no more help. Try yer luck at the tannery."

Hodgins opened his coat briefly to show his badge. "Already have a job. Where's the boss?"

The driver looked at the badge, and then spit a large wad of chewing tobacco into a pile of snow beside Hodgins. Most of it landed in the snow, sinking in a few inches, a trail of slim hanging down the side. Some of the spittle hit Hodgins' left boot. The driver watched as Hodgins casually shoved his boot into some clean snow to remove the mess.

"Office is on the second floor." He pointed to a staircase leading up to a door, then turned back to his wagon.

Hodgins stopped at the foot of the stairs. It looked like they'd used the worst pieces of lumber available to build them. He put one foot on the first step and grabbed the railing. The step bowed under his weight and the railing shifted. He took a deep breath and quickly ascended, trying not to think about the wobbling under his feet. There was a sign nailed to the door that read *Office*. Hodgins lifted the latch and opened the door.

"State yer business." It took a moment for Hodgins to find the source of the voice. He closed the door, shutting out the bright sunlight, allowing his eyes to adjust to the dimness that remained. The room had no windows, just a few lanterns hanging on nails driven into the walls. They provided little illumination. "I said, state yer business. I'm busy and can't wait all day."

A scrawny man sat behind a table that was being used as a desk. There was a lantern and ledger-book in the middle, with an inkwell on one side and a cup of tea on the other.

"I'm Detective Hodgins. I need to speak with you about an incident involving Fred Walker. Are you in charge?"

The man pushed the ledger away and motioned to a chair near the desk. It looked like it had been made from the same wood as the stairs. Hodgins remained standing.

"Name's Horace Harmon. I run the place. Haven't seen Walker in weeks. That's gratitude for you. Promote the man, he gets into a fight, and then up and disappears. If you see him, tell him he's fired."

"Tell me about this fight."

"Why don't you ask him yourself?" Harmon asked.

"Can't. He's dead. Now, about the fight?"

"What? Oh, yes. Dead you say? How?"

"That's what I'm *trying* to find out. Who did he fight with?"

Harmon got up and walked over to a door at the back that Hodgins hadn't noticed. He opened it and the smell of freshly cut wood filled the room. Harmon stepped out onto a walkway. Hodgins followed.

Harmon looked around then pointed. "There," he yelled over the noise of the saws. "John Richardson."

"I'll need to speak with him. Can I use your office?"

Harmon mumbled something Hodgins couldn't make out, but agreed. He went down a staircase that led to the mill, and came back with a tall, muscular man, who appeared to be in his mid-twenties.

"This here detective needs a word with you."

"A detective you say? I'm honoured." Richardson bowed slightly.

Hodgins took an instant dislike to Richardson, with his cocky, smug smile. He could tell from the young man's tone he thought quite well of himself. They all went into the office and Harmon closed the door, muffling the sounds from below.

Hodgins turned to Harmon. "I prefer to conduct my interviews in private, if you don't mind."

"Begging your pardon, but I feel I owe it to my employee to stay. I've heard how members of the constabulary bully confessions out of innocent people. This is my business and my office. Either I stay, or you leave."

The two men stared at each other for a minute before Hodgins spoke. "I understand it's actually Mr. Flanagan's business. You are just his employee."

"Well, yes, but . . ." Harmon blustered.

Hodgins reached out with his right arm. His hand pressed against Harmon's chest, pinning him against the wall. His face so close to Harmon's their noses almost touched. "Stay if you must, but don't interrupt." Hodgins released Harmon, turned and walked behind the desk straightening his jacket and then sat in Harmon's chair.

Richardson started to laugh. "I like you Detective.

Now what can I do to assist you?"

Hodgins took the small black notebook out of his pocket, placed it on the desk and flipped it open to a blank page. He glanced over at Harmon, who stood by the door. He scowled at Hodgins, but didn't move. His arms hung down at his side, his balding scalp shimmered in the light from the lantern hanging on the wall over his head. The few stringy hairs he had dangled over his eyes. Hodgins picked up the quill pen and dipped it in the ink well. He could feel Harmon's glare from across the room.

Hodgins wrote the date on the top of the page, then looked up at Richardson. "Fred Walker. I hear you didn't like him much."

The smile was instantly replaced by a scowl. "Cocky little git."

Hodgins made a few scribbles in his book. "Tell me about the fight a few months ago."

Richardson waved his hand as though dismissing the comment. "He was promoted to foreman and was bragging to everyone how he was so much better than me. I should've been promoted, not Fred." He turned to Harmon. "And I was right. Fred stopped coming to work weeks ago." Turning back to Hodgins he said, "I'm foreman now." The cocky smile returned. "Can't wait to rub that bit of news in his face."

Hodgins made a few more notes, and while writing said, "I'm afraid you won't get the chance." He stopped writing and looked directly at Richardson. "He's dead."

"Hmm, shame. I was rather looking forward to telling him I was given his job."

Hodgins dipped the quill and wrote a few more things in his book. He helped himself to a piece of Harmon's blotting paper before closing the notebook. "I guess that's all for now." He got up and walked over to Harmon.

"Thank you for the use of your office. Might I impose a bit longer? I'd like to talk to some of your other employees. I'll just walk around the mill and chat with a few. Won't take them away from their work long."

Harmon said nothing, but opened the back door, allowing the detective to exit into the mill.

Hodgins walked around the saw mill, chatting with several of the workers. It was the same with each man; they listened to his questions, and then looked up at the walkway. Harmon and Richardson were standing side by side, watching Hodgins. One by one, each man shook his head and went back to work without answering one question.

Hodgins' frustration built. No one would talk to him. They were too scared to speak. *Is it Harmon, or Richardson, they are all afraid of? Or both?* A shrill whistle interrupted his thoughts. The machinery slowed to a stop and most of the men started to exit the mill. Hodgins pulled out his pocket watch and checked the time. Lunch break. He looked up at the walkway and nodded at Harmon and Richardson, then followed the men out of the mill and continued down to the tavern to meet Barnes.

CHAPTER 7

Hodgins was a block from the tavern when he spotted Barnes crossing the road from the opposite direction. Hodgins called to him, and Barnes waited at the entrance. The constable opened the tavern door and held it for the detective. Hodgins pointed to an empty table in the far corner and they weaved their way over. One of the servers hustled to the table.

"Nice to see you again, Sir," the server said. Hodgins smiled at the pretty brunette. "What can I get you today?"

"The Cottage Pie was quite delicious. I think I'll have that again. And bring us a pot of Darjeeling tea. It was quite nice as well."

"I'll have the Cottage Pie too," Barnes said.

The server hurried off while the men removed their coats and settled in. Just as they got comfortable, she was back with the tea. She balanced the tray in her left hand, and dragged a damp towel across the table with her right. She put the tea pot in the centre of the table, placed a cup in front of each man and then hurried off again.

"Hope you had better luck than I did," Hodgins said.

Barnes opened his new notebook to the first page. Hodgins noticed how far through the book the pages changed from worn to fresh. He was impressed at the copious notes taken.

"After you went to the mill I walked a bit farther and came across the post office. I figured everybody in town goes in there."

"Good thinking," Hodgins said.

"There were several young ladies there. Turns out they were friends of Miss Smythe, er, Mrs. Flanagan. They all said pretty much the same thing. They met Emily through the church shortly after the family moved here from England. Seems they were all sweet on Fred, and couldn't believe she married Flanagan instead. I didn't tell them what happened to Mr. Walker. Was that wrong of me Sir?

Hodgins thought it over and said, "No, probably just as well. If they were that fond of him they may have become hysterical or something. Is that all they told you?"

"I got the impression that one of them may know something more, but didn't want to say in front of her friends. A Miss Penelope Cooke. I think I should try to talk to her alone. Maybe after lunch?"

"Maybe," Hodgins said. "What else?"

"After the post office, I walked a bit farther before coming back this way. Figured I might try my luck with the minister who married them. Found him in the Presbyterian church." He flipped the pages. "A Reverend Baker. Said it was most peculiar. Just the two families. The Reverend said he normally didn't perform weddings like that, but both Mr. Smythe and Mr. Flanagan were large contributors."

Barnes looked up at Hodgins. "Guess even the clergy recognize class distinction, eh Sir?" he said with a grin, but Hodgins wasn't listening.

Barnes turned around trying to see what had the detective's attention.

A young man stood just inside the doorway. Pulling a wool cap off his head, he glanced around the room, twisting it in his hands. When he looked in Hodgins direction, the detective stood and waved the man over.

"It's Will Greene, isn't it?" Hodgins asked.

Will nodded, but said nothing. He just stood beside the table looking around.

Barnes reached across to the next table and pulled over an empty chair. Greene slid onto the seat and slouched down. Hodgins and Barnes waited.

"I can't let them see me here," Greene finally said. He

looked around again. "I saw you come in and followed. He hesitated, then spoke quickly. "He beat him real bad, Richardson did. Thought he was going to kill him. Fred Walker, I mean. Couple of the guys had to pull him off Fred. You don't cross John Richardson."

The door to the tavern opened and Green's head snapped around, looking to see who came in. It was no one he knew, so he turned back to Hodgins. "He thought it was Fred's fault he didn't get promoted. When he found out it was Fred what was made foreman, well he just blew up. John harassed Fred every day. Messed things up and blamed Fred. Richardson's done everything he could think of to get on Mr. Harman's good side and make Fred look bad. Haven't seen Fred since the Christmas dance."

Greene stood, pushing the chair into the man sitting at the next table. He looked around nervously, twisting the wool cap again. "Gotta go. Mr. Harman sometimes comes in for a beer at lunch. He can't see me with you." He took one final look around, and darted out the door.

"That was odd," Barnes said.

"Not really." Hodgins flipped through his notebook until he found the few comments he made when he spoke to Greene in the mill. He made a little star and printed a tiny comment between the lines.

"I had the impression he wanted to tell me something

earlier, but was afraid to say anything. The man he mentioned, Richardson, that's the bloke who fought with Walker. A real blow-hard." He paused. "So, who do I believe? Greene and Richardson told totally opposite stories. Richardson said that Walker bragged about getting promoted. Just because I don't like Richardson doesn't make him a liar."

"True, Sir." Barnes paused to collect his thoughts. "The people I spoke to today, they all liked Fred Walker. If he was a braggart, I don't believe so many people would be all that fond of him."

Hodgins tapped his pencil on the tabletop. "Maybe. Maybe not. People have been known to fool others. That's how con-men work. Charm you out of your life savings. I'm not saying Walker was like that. Greene was convincing though."

"So how do we find out who's telling the truth?"

"Keep talking to people. There must be other folk who like or dislike the two men."

The server came back with their food, and Hodgins and Barnes dug in. It didn't take long for Barnes to devour his Cottage Pie.

"Good, isn't it?" Hodgins said. "I think it's even better than last time."

Barnes nodded and mumbled as he scooped the last

few bits onto his fork and shovelled it into his mouth. Hodgins watched as the constable took a swig of tea, swished it around in his mouth, and then swallowed with a contented sigh.

"That was perfect," Barnes said. "Fills you up and takes the chill right out of your bones. Is your wife a good cook, if you don't mind me asking?"

Hodgins smiled. "She's a very good cook. It's a wonder I can still fit into my clothes. A very good cook indeed."

Hodgins glanced at the table behind Barnes and swore. "When did he come in?"

"Who?"

"Horace Harmon. The man running Flanagan's mill. Good thing that lad left when he did."

Hodgins signaled for the server, who was standing at the bar. They settled their bill and went outside.

"There, Sir. That's one of the young ladies I spoke to at the post office, Miss Cooke." Barnes pointed at an attractive lady across the road.

"I'm certain she wanted to tell me something about Mrs. Flanagan."

Hodgins looked at the woman, then at Barnes, who was staring at her - a big, silly grin on his face.

The corner of Hodgins' mouth curled up. "Pretty,

isn't she?"

"What?" Barnes stammered and blushed. "Oh, yes. I hadn't noticed."

Hodgins laughed loud enough that the young lady turned. She saw Barnes and waved. Barnes waved back.

"Go, see what she knows. Be back here by three. There's a train at 3:15." Barnes was half way across the street by the time Hodgins finished speaking.

Hodgins wandered through the town stopping at some of the shops and businesses asking about Walker and Richardson. Most were too busy to talk, and the rest didn't tell him anything he didn't already know.

CHAPTER 8

Wednesday evening Hodgins sat in the front room with his wife and father-in-law, going over the outcome of the inquest. The proceedings took less than an hour, and there really wasn't anything new to tell Cordelia.

"The two boys who found the body, Michael and Danny, were asked to repeat how they happened to find Walker." He laughed when he told her about Barnes' testimony.

"He had his notebook, the one he bought afterwards, and flipped through the pages as though reminding himself what happened. The judge had no idea that Barnes hadn't taken any notes at the time."

"How could he not have taken notes?"

"Oh, I guess I didn't tell you about that. He had a receipt stuffed in one of his pockets, and scribbled a few things on the back. That was his report."

Cordelia couldn't hold back her giggles, despite her husband's frown.

"I'm sorry, Dear. I know how particular you are about police reports. You must have been furious."

Hodgins nodded, and then smiled. "He did seem quite professional on the stand. The lad learns quick. Have to give him that."

He walked over to the fireplace and gave the logs a few pokes. "After Dr. McKenzie gave his report and explained the wounds, it was obvious to everyone it was foul play. I didn't need an inquest to tell me that."

"So what's next?" Harold asked. "Does anything change with your investigation?"

"No. I've been going on the assumption of murder all along. Now that the inquest is over, it's officially murder and not speculation. By not waiting I've gained a week. Got to people while things were fresh in their minds. If they knew it was a murder investigation, they may not have been so forthcoming with information."

"Do you have to make many more trips to Stouffville?" Cordelia asked.

"Probably a few more. Going tomorrow as it happens. Walker's body was released after the hearing and his cousin mentioned they'll be having the funeral tomorrow afternoon. I thought I'd attend, observe the mourners. See if anyone seems suspicious or out of place.

Cordelia's mother joined them and talk instantly

changed from murder to the social set; something Euphemia found acceptable for mixed company. She nattered on for over an hour before Hodgins excused himself and went upstairs for the night.

* * *

The next day Hodgins found himself in the little village of Stouffville once more. The St. James Presbyterian Church was overflowing with mourners. Standing just inside the door, he took in all the faces. He recognized several of the mill workers gathered together in the back corner. Up at the front of the church he spotted the Lowes. George seemed to be comforting a young man and women. He turned his head and saw Hodgins standing at the back. He touched his wife's arm and nodded towards Hodgins. The Flanagans and Smythes were also at the front. The large turnout seemed to validate what Will Greene had told him at the tavern. Fred Walker appeared to be quite popular. It was becoming more evident that Richardson's story was a complete fabrication. If Walker was as petty and mean as Richardson indicated, Hodgins doubted the church would be so full.

"Detective?"

Hodgins turned to find Will standing behind him. He reached out and shook Greene's hand.

"I see there are a lot of mill workers here," Hodgins

said.

"Yes. Mr. Flanagan shut the mill for the service."

Hodgins raised one eyebrow. "Really? He doesn't strike me as the sort to let a funeral stop business."

Greene snorted. "Don't think it was out of compassion or respect. Makes him look good. We can't go to the cemetery for the burial. It's straight back to the mill." He looked down as his old, dirty clothing. "I'd never come into a church looking like this, but I can't wear my good suit at the mill, and we don't have time to go home and change. Harmon will make sure we all head back soon as the service is over."

Greene started to move towards his friends, then stepped back. "Fred was real nice. I hope you find the bastard and hang him." Satisfied he'd said his piece, Green joined the other mill workers in the corner.

The look of hate that showed in Greene's eyes was brief, but it convinced Hodgins that it was probably Richardson who'd been kicking up a fuss at the mill. He reached into his pocket for his notebook and hesitated. He decided it wouldn't be right to make notes inside the church, so he slipped outside and stood at the bottom of the steps, out of the way of the people coming in. He jotted a note to check on Richardson's character and background, then went back inside.

The service lasted about thirty minutes; several young women cried throughout. When it was over, everyone filed out and either got into buggies and wagons, or went on foot, to the cemetery. Hodgins saw Harmon herding the mill workers like cattle in the opposite direction, back to the mill. Waiting for everyone to leave the church, Hodgins then followed to the cemetery, keeping a little distance between himself and the mourners. A black buggy went past, pulled by a large chestnut horse. He recognized the driver as Reverend Baker.

The mourners assembled around an open grave. Hodgins wormed his way through the crowd until he was close enough to the Flanagans to hear their conversation. Both were watching as the plain pine coffin was lowered into the ground.

"Stop your sniffling, Emily," Flanagan whispered. "You're making a spectacle of yourself. A married woman carrying on like that. What will people think?"

"He was my friend, Patrick. An old and dear friend. We grew up together. I don't care what people think."

"Do you think he ever suspected your little secret?"

Emily gasped and turned to say something to her husband when she spotted Hodgins. She touched Flanagan's arm. "Hush."

Hodgins smiled at Emily and removed his hat.

73

Flanagan turned around to see what Emily was concerned about. "What the hell are you doing here?" he bellowed. All heads turned.

Flanagan's face turned red and his eyes narrowed. "Can't you give us one day of peace?"

Hodgins shrugged. "Just paying my respects."

A soft murmur filled the air as people whispered among themselves, trying to figure out who the stranger was and why Flanagan was upset at his presence.

Reverend Baker moved to the head of the grave and everyone quieted down. Hodgins looked around and noticed several people staring at him. Most looked away, embarrassed, but one man kept eye contact for several seconds.

After Fred Walker was laid to rest, Hodgins watched as Emily walked over to the Lowes and spoke to the young man and woman he saw at the church. He was too far away to hear what was said, but Emily gave them both a long hug before leaving with her husband. George and Grace Lowe noticed Hodgins and walked over to speak to him, leaving the two young people at the graveside.

"Do you have news?" George asked.

Hodgins shook his head. "We're still following up leads. Nothing definite yet."

Someone watched them. He recognized the man as

the one who kept eye contact with him earlier.

"Who's that man there?" he asked.

Both Lowes turned to see. "Oh, that's Mr. Carter. He's not quite right in the head."

"Grace," George exclaimed.

Ignoring her husband's annoyance she continued. "He's really harmless. Kicked in the head a few years ago by a horse. Hasn't been the same since. Doesn't say much, just stares mostly."

She stopped talking long enough to call to the young man and woman to join them and then turned back to Hodgins.

"Fred's brother and sister. George telegraphed them yesterday. Sent one to their father too. He's still in England.

Grace moved between the two newcomers, placing one arm around each. "This is Anabelle and Henry. And this nice man is Detective Hodgins. He's going to find out who did this terrible thing to Fred."

"We're doing our best. I'm very sorry for your loss."

Anabelle gave Hodgins a weak smile. Her eyes were red from crying. Henry appeared angry.

"This is your best?" Henry waved his arms in frustration. "Why aren't you trying to find the fiend who murdered my brother?"

George placed a hand on Henry's shoulder. "That's not fair, Henry. The detective has been here several times trying to get to the bottom of this."

Henry's face turned red. "I'm sorry. It's just hard to understand why anyone would kill Fred. Everyone liked him. I can't believe he's really gone."

Anabelle started to weep. Henry put his arm around her shoulder and led her a few steps away.

"You'll join us at the house Detective Hodgins?" Grace inquired.

"No, but thank you. I still have plenty of work to do." He tipped his hat and headed back to the train station.

CHAPTER 9

Hodgins spent the next morning at the waterfront. He quickly scanned the area around the train tracks and road before wiggling the loose boards on one of the deserted buildings near Connors Wharf. Two of the buildings west of the wharf were deserted and he wondered if they played a part in the mystery surrounding Walker's murder.

He almost had the board removed when he heard voices. Hodgins released the plank and stepped around the corner out of view. He heard enough of their conversation to figure out one was an estate agent, and the other a client.

The men stopped at the corner of the building when they noticed Hodgins. "Wouldn't waste my time looking at that pile of scrap," the estate agent said. "Better buildings than that available down here." He handed a business card to Hodgins and continued up to the road.

Hodgins read the card before stuffing it into his

pocket. Alexander Robertson, Estate Agent, 489 Church Street, Toronto. *Might come in handy later*, he thought.

The wind had picked up and was blowing the snow around. Hodgins tightened his scarf and decided to retreat to the warmth of the records office again. He recalled reading something on his last visit, but couldn't remember what it was. He was sure it was relevant and needed to find it.

He found what he was looking for and returned to the station. Hodgins copied the list of properties he gathered from his two visits to the records office from his notebook to the blackboard. He sat on the edge of his desk and faced the board. He was still slightly irritated that he hadn't been able to get that loose board off the window to peek in. Hodgins was more frustrated after his new discovery at the records office.

"Damn, damn, damn," he muttered as he slammed his notebook closed and dropped it on the desk.

Hodgins stood and started pacing, stopping periodically to read what he had printed on the blackboard, cursing under his breath. Flanagan owned one factory and several homes in a seamy part of the city.

"Working late, Sir?"

Hodgins looked up to see Barnes standing behind him, overcoat buttoned, scarf tightly wrapped around his neck.

"Late? Is it?" Hodgins pulled out his pocket watch. "Hmm, 7:13. Guess it is late." He tucked the watch back into his vest pocket, picked his notebook off his desk and grabbed his coat from the back of his chair. He breezed past Barnes without further comment, buttoning his coat as he went.

Staring out the windows of the trolley all the way home, Hodgins mulled over the day's discoveries. When he arrived, he hung up his coat, went straight to the front room, and dragged one of the chairs closer to the fireplace. He slouched down and stretched his lanky legs towards the flames. Heat slowly crept through his soles and up his legs, gradually warming him up.

Sara came running in. "Daddy, you're home." She tried to climb into his lap, but he pushed her off.

"Daddy's tired."

She stood beside the chair quietly, but Hodgins barely acknowledged her. Pouting, she ran back to the kitchen where Cordelia and Euphemia prepared dinner. Hodgins didn't hear his wife. He jumped when she touched his shoulder.

"Where is your mind Bertie? I've called you three times.

"Sorry dear, my mind was elsewhere."

"That's obvious. Even Sara noticed."

Hodgins rose from the chair and followed Cordelia down the hall and into the dining room. All through dinner he mumbled and grunted. He yelped when Cordelia kicked his ankle.

"Mother asked you a question."

He looked from his wife to Euphemia, who sat glaring at him. A quick look around the table told him just how poorly he had been behaving. Sara fought back tears, and his father-in-law's usual jovial look was replaced with a furrowed brow and concern.

"I do apologize. This case is so puzzling. I just can't stop thinking about it."

He picked up his napkin and jotted his mouth.

"The meal was delicious, but I'm not terribly hungry. Please excuse me."

He dropped the napkin on his plate, covering the remains of his barely touched meal, and got up from the table. He went down the hall and retrieved his notebook from his coat pocket, then went upstairs to his room.

He removed his suit jacket and vest, taking care to hang them in the wardrobe. He crossed to the washstand in the corner and splashed water on his face. Feeling a little rejuvenated, he went to the davenport that was nestled beside the bedroom window. Hodgins rolled the chair out and sat down. He opened the book and re-read his notes, starting with the comments he copied off Barnes' receipt. The bedroom door opened as Hodgins rolled out more wick on the oil lamp.

"You've not been yourself all evening, Bertie. Mother's been grumbling about your lack of manners." Cordelia stood behind Hodgins trying to see what he was reading. "Is it the young man those two boys found?"

Hodgins covered his mouth as he yawned. "It's become very frustrating." He pushed the notebook aside. "I have a couple of possible suspects, but I can't find anything to point directly at either." He got up and started pacing around the room.

Cordelia moved over to her vanity, out of his way. She removed the pins from her hair and started to undo the plaiting, running her fingers though to smooth out any snarls. She then picked up the tortoiseshell comb and slowly ran it through her wavy hair. Satisfied it was tangle-free, Cordelia picked up the matching boar-hair brush and started her daily routine; one hundred strokes every evening and every morning.

"Tell me what you know. Maybe if you say it aloud something will fall into place. Who do you think may have killed him? What was his name? Fred something?"

"Walker. His name is Fred Walker. He was only

twenty six." Hodgins went back to the davenport to retrieve his notebook.

"Quite often it turns out to be someone the victim knew. Patrick Flanagan is still at the top of my list."

Cordelia stopped brushing and looked at her husband's reflection in the mirror. "Who is Patrick Flanagan?"

Hodgins sat at the end of their bed and placed the notebook beside him. "He's Emily's husband."

He held up his hand in anticipation of Cordelia's questions. "Emily is the woman Fred wanted to marry."

Cordelia smiled. "A love triangle? How interesting. Tell me more."

"Fred and Emily were friends when they lived in England. Sweethearts more like. Fred's mother died and when his father re-married, Fred and his siblings were sent here to live with a relative. Emily's family moved here too, but only a few years ago. Don't know why, yet."

"I assume Emily and Fred started courting after she moved?" Cordelia forgot all about her evening routine and moved over to the bed beside her husband. "Why did she marry this Flanagan fellow?"

Hodgins shrugged. "Don't know that either. Do know it was sudden. Secret too."

"A rushed wedding? You know what that usually

means?"

Hodgins laughed. "Yes. Fred's cousin suggested as much. Correction. His cousin's wife. You'd like her. She loves to gossip."

Cordelia stood up, placing her hands on her hips. "Bertie, are you saying I gossip?"

"Uh, no," he stammered. "I'd never . . ."

Cordelia laughed. "I'm only teasing. Go on."

"Flanagan practically threw Fred out of the house Christmas day. That's when Fred found out Emily was married. Flanagan was also seen arguing with Fred on the train. Far as I can tell, that's the last anyone saw of Fred. And Flanagan lied about not seeing Fred after Christmas."

Hodgins paced again. "Fred worked at the local mill. He was promoted to foreman in November. Guess who owns the mill."

"Patrick Flanagan?"

Hodgins nodded. Cordelia moved back to her vanity and resumed brushing her hair. "But if this Flanagan person had already married Emily, why kill him?"

"Because Emily was still in love with Fred. It was evident from her reaction when she found out. Flanagan is much older. Maybe he thought Emily would eventually leave him and run off with Walker."

Cordelia finished brushing her hair and started

removing the layers of clothing so she could slip into her night dress. "You said you have a couple of suspects."

"Yes, a man about Walker's age. John Richardson. He was quite angry that Fred was promoted instead of him. Actually beat Fred pretty bad."

Hodgins picked up the notebook and flipped through the pages until he found the notes he'd made while talking with Dr. McKenzie. Cordelia came over and unbuttoned his shirt.

"It's late. Maybe if you sleep on it, it will fall together." She took the notebook from him and glanced at the sketch of the peculiar bruise. "Why did you draw a bird?"

Hodgins draped his shirt over the back of the chair and turned to face her. "Bird? What are you talking about?"

She pointed at the sketch. "Here."

Hodgins noticed she was holding the book upside down. He took it from her and turned it around a few times, looking at the sketch from all angles. "A bird. The bruise looks like a bloody bird. What the devil would have left a mark like that?"

He looked at Cordelia. "Instead of helping, you've just thrown another mystery into the jumble."

CHAPTER 10

Next morning at the station house, Hodgins found an envelope on his desk. His name and rank were written in fancy script. *Detective Albert Hodgins*. No address – no stamp – no post mark. He turned it over and slipped his thumb under the flap to open it. A loud crash across the room startled him. Swearing under his breath he stuck his thumb in his mouth, sucking at the fresh paper cut. He looked up and saw Barnes bent down picking up the items he'd knocked to the floor.

Hodgins dropped the bloodied envelope back on the desk and yelled, "Barnes."

The constable looked up. Hodgins waved him over. Barnes placed the metal tray and papers back on the desk he shared with another constable, then hurried over to the detective.

"Sir?"

"Go fetch the evidence box with Walker's belongings."

Barnes scurried to the back room and appeared at the doorway five minutes later, carrying a large cardboard box with 'FRED WALKER 07 JAN 1874' printed in large letters across the side. He winced as his knuckles scrapped the door frame when he tried to squeeze through. Barnes turned sideways and slid past without any further injuries. Huffing, he dropped the box onto Hodgins' desk. Removing the lid, Hodgins leaned it against the box and started pulling out the contents.

"Oh, that's rank." Barnes waved his hand in front of his face and took a step back.

Hodgins wrinkled his nose. "I guess the box was packed before the things were dry. Clothing does tend to hold onto smells when put away wet. Add the fishy lake water and . . . well, you just experienced it. Puts me in mind of the first time I went fishing with my older brother. I was so proud of my fish that I wanted to keep it as long as possible. Hid it under my bed. That smell lingered all summer." He gestured towards the chair in front of his desk. "Sit down, Constable. We need to go over everything and try to figure out what we've missed."

"Me, Sir?"

Hodgins nodded. "Yes, you. You were first on the scene. It was a sloppy job, but you've done some excellent investigating since."

"Thank you, Sir. I've tried my best."

Hodgins moved his tray, inkwell, and pen into his drawer, put the few other items from his desk on his chair in order to clear the top, and then slipped the unopened letter into his jacket pocket. He spread out Walker's belongings; a long overcoat, overalls, smock, felt lumberman boots, small key, coins, train ticket, and shirt. He placed a pearl cufflink on top of the grey work shirt and slid it in front of Barnes.

Barnes whistled. "Expensive looking cufflink. Must have cost a small fortune." He looked puzzled. "Where did it come from? I don't remember seeing it before."

"Guess I didn't mention it. Remember last Saturday when you came to fetch me? Ben Grove and his youngest boy brought it in. Seems the lad picked it up from beside the body. Don't even know if it has anything to do with Walker." Hodgins tapped the shirt with one finger. "What do you see? Do these two things go together?"

Barnes picked up the cufflink and examined it. He turned it over a few times and held it up into the ray of light that drifted across the room through the frosted window. He shook his head.

"No, they belong to different people. He picked up the shirt. "The fabric is rough. Belongs to a working man. The cufflink was bought by someone with money. Some labourers might have one set of cufflinks for their Sunday best, but he wouldn't of had it when working."

He put it back on the desk and placed the cufflink beside it. "A working man's cufflink would be plain. Probably silver, not gold like this one. Besides," he lifted the sleeve. "This one has button cuffs. Why would there be a cufflink on him?"

"Very good." Hodgins picked up the cufflink let it roll to the centre of his palm. "If this was just lying beside Walker's body by chance, it would most likely have been dropped recently. What are the odds someone who could afford such an expensive piece of jewellery would be strolling around the docks in his finery?"

"I've never seen a toff on the docks anytime I was walking my beat, Sir."

"Exactly. So for now, let's work on the assumption it was dropped by the murderer. Who is on our suspect list that can afford this?"

Barnes smiled. "Mr. Flanagan." He paused to think about it. "Oh." The smile vanished. "How do we prove it? I didn't see any initials on it."

Hodgins shrugged and started putting the items back in the box. "I think we need to go for a walk."

"Sir?"

"I was down at the wharf yesterday and saw a couple

of vacant buildings. Turns out one belongs to Flanagan, and it wasn't locked. I feel it's our duty to check on it. Make sure no one's been using it and causing damage."

Barnes looked at the ceiling for a moment, nose crinkled, left eye closed. His mouth dropped and his eye opened as it dawned on him. "Yes, we'll have to thoroughly examine inside the building. Might just turn up something interesting," he said.

* * *

Hodgins pointed at the last building beside the side rail. It was deserted and even from a distance you could see the boards over the windows were loose, some starting to split.

"That one there belongs to Flanagan. Missed it the first time I went through the records. It's registered under his wife's name. According to the city records, he rented it to an import company for a few years, but it's been sitting empty since this summer past. From the looks of the building, I'd say whatever Flanagan was charging for rent was too much. I wouldn't pay one cent for a building this run down."

Hodgins and Barnes stepped over the tracks carefully, trying not to slip in the fresh snow. It had been snowing most of the morning, and it was undisturbed around that section of track. None of the trains had gone down the side rail that morning and the snow had accumulated a fair bit, resulting in the bottoms of their trousers becoming wet and heavy.

"Look, Sir." Barnes pointed at the large sliding door at the front of the building. "Footprints."

Hodgins stopped beside Barnes and looked at the trail of prints coming down from the road, across the tracks, into the building, and back again.

"Interesting." Hodgins smiled. "I'm sure Mr. Flanagan would want us to check it out. Make sure everything is in order."

The sliding door was slightly ajar, so Barnes walked over and peeked in. "Too dark to see anything. All the windows have been shuttered."

Hodgins had already gone over to the closest window, removed the board he had previously loosened, and worked at prying the shutters open. The wood was cheap and well weathered, giving way with little effort and allowing light to shine in.

Barnes slid the door open, making the building brighter inside. "There's another door at the back. I'll open it, then it we should be able to see well enough to have a good look 'round. Seems pretty empty though, so it shouldn't take too long."

By the time Barnes had the back door open Hodgins

was already looking through a pile of blankets in the corner.

"Probably just some vagrant come in to sleep last night," Barnes said.

Hodgins turned. "How long has it been snowing?"

"Two or three hours."

"Right. So if someone came in last night, before it started to snow, would there be tracks going in both directions?"

Barnes wrinkled his nose and brow while he thought. "No. There would only be one set going out."

"So?"

"Someone was here right before us." Barnes looked puzzled. "But wouldn't we have seen him?"

Hodgins walked to the sliding door, indicating for Barnes to follow.

"The snow was heavy earlier, and now it's eased off. Look at the footprints."

Barnes knelt down beside the prints. "The tracks are half filled in. Whoever it was must have been here 'bout a half hour or more ago." He stood and brushed the snow from his trousers.

"Correct. You're looking, but you haven't been seeing. You need to observe and absorb everything. You should have realized right off that the tracks were fresh, but not immediately left." Hodgins put his hand on Barnes' shoulder. "Stop rushing. The smallest thing could be crucial."

They went back inside and looked around the empty room. There was nothing in the pile of blankets, and the lone desk by the front window didn't even have one piece of paper left in it. They started to follow the tracks, wondering who was in the building that morning and why. Was it just a vagrant looking for a place to rest, or did someone come in and remove a piece of evidence? Was the building even tied to the murder? Hodgins wondered if they were wasting their time pursing this particular avenue.

CHAPTER 11

Hodgins was continually jostled on the busy streetcar Saturday morning, his thoughts about Richardson disrupted every time his foot was trod on. He was finding it difficult to piece everything together. Was Richardson the one who ended the life of Fred Walker? Was a promotion at work enough of a motive? *People have killed for less, and he was certainly petty enough.*

Hodgins's disdain for Richardson grew every time his name came up. Everyone seemed to confirm his initial opinion; the man was too arrogant, too cocky. *Doesn't make him a murderer though.* By the time Hodgins arrived at the front of the station, he'd made up his mind to find out all he could about Mr. John Richardson.

It was still early and very quiet in the station house. The lads on the night shift were doing the last of their paperwork, and not many of the day shift had arrived. He could hear mumbling in the tiny kitchen towards the back. Some would be having a final cup of tea before heading out into the cool winter air, while others would be trying to warm up before starting for the day.

Hodgins could see someone in the Inspector's office. *Must be important to get the Inspector up so early.* From the cut of the coat, the visitor had money. Hodgins walked to his desk to see if there had been any messages left for him. Since there was nothing, he told the desk Sergeant he was going back to Stouffville to poke around, and would be back mid-afternoon.

He walked down to Union Station and was pleased to find a train almost ready. He had just enough time to purchase his ticket and then buy the morning edition from a newsboy working the platform. The train was half empty, so he settled by a window, away from other passengers and opened the paper.

"Ticket, Sir."

Hodgins put down the paper and took his train ticket from his pocket. He recognized the conductor immediately.

"Good morning, Detective. Ticket please."

Hodgins smiled at the conductor's memory, and decided to press for some more information. "Good morning. I remember you said your son worked at the mill with Mr. Walker. I assume he is also acquainted with Mr. Richardson?"

"Yes, he knows him. It's a small town. Everyone

knows everybody, even if only in passing."

"So, you know him too?"

The conductor smiled. "In passing."

"Do you recall if he was on the train when you saw Mr. Walker and Mr. Flanagan arguing?"

"No, Sir. I didn't see him that day. I don't believe I've ever seen him on the train. But I don't work every train."

He punched the ticket, handed it back to Hodgins, and continued down the aisle.

Hodgins sighed and went back to the newspaper, hoping the distraction would clear his mind. He'd discovered a long time ago that the harder he tried to think about something the more frustrated he got. Once he relaxed and put his mind to something trivial, he would have some sort of revelation. Didn't seem to be working today.

Having finished the paper by the time the train pulled into Stouffville station, Hodgins left it on the seat for someone else to read. He stepped onto the platform, took a few steps, and stopped. He really didn't know where he wanted to go first. It was unlike him to head out without some sort of plan.

"Can I be of assistance, Detective?"

Hodgins turned and found himself looking at the train conductor again.

"No, I'm all right, Mister . . . ?"

"Jones, Sir."

"Mr. Jones. Just trying to gather my thoughts."

"If it's Richardson you're wanting, he's probably at the mill. Saturday's their busiest day."

"Thank you Mr. Jones. I'll keep that in mind." Hodgins nodded and walked towards the main road. He automatically turned right without giving any thought as to where he was going, then realized he was headed to the Lowe's. George Lowe was clearing the snow off the front walk, and waved when he saw Hodgins.

"Do you have news, Detective?"

"No, we're still investigating."

"Oh, I see." The look of disappointment was heart-breaking. Lowe cleared the last bit of snow and invited Hodgins inside. They settled in front of the fire in the sitting room. Hodgins pulled out his notebook, flipped through a few pages skimming his notes, then looked up at Lowe.

"What can you tell me about John Richardson? Was the fight with your cousin unusual?"

"John? Is he the one who fought with Fred? Well, he was always a bit of a bully. Hardly a week went by when someone wasn't talking about him. During grade school most of the boys around here got at least one black eye from him. When he starting working he never stayed at one job very long. Always thought he knew more than the boss. Seemed to settle a bit when he went to the mill though."

Hodgins added the information to his notes, and thanked Lowe for his time. He was putting his notebook away when Mrs. Lowe scurried into the room.

"I thought I heard voices. George, why didn't you tell me we had company?"

Before he could respond, she turned to Hodgins.

"Detective, sit back down and let me fetch tea and biscuits." She turned and headed towards the kitchen.

"Thank you Mrs. Lowe, but I really must be going. It's very kind of you but there are other people I need to speak to this morning."

She stopped and turned back to Hodgins and her husband. "It won't take but a minute."

"Thank you, but it's imperative that I gather as much information as I can so we can find out who killed Mr. Walker. If either of you think of anything further, please send a note to me at the police station."

After leaving the Lowe residence, he headed towards the mill. As he crossed the road to go inside, he could hear yelling. It was loud enough that Hodgins was almost able to make out the words over the sound of the saws. He walked through the large sliding doors at the front and spotted Richardson lambasting one of the workers. His face was inches from the young man, and he was poking the worker in the chest to emphasize his point. The young man cringed each time that finger jabbed him.

Hodgins stormed over and tapped Richardson hard on the shoulder. "Excuse me. Might I have a word?"

Richardson flew around, fist in the air ready to strike. The young man gasped. Hodgins didn't flinch.

Richardson stopped as soon as he saw who it was. He flexed his hand and dropped his arm. The smile that crossed his face was more like a grimace.

"Detective. To what do I owe this pleasure?"

Hodgins reminded himself to be civil. "A word please. Can we step outside"

"Of course. Anything to help the police." As Hodgins turned to follow Richardson outside, he noticed the look of relief on the young man's face.

"What can I do for you, Detective?"

"Just tying up a few loose ends. Can you tell me where you were January fifth and sixth?"

"I was in Peterborough. My sister got married on the third. Had a family gathering of sorts. I was there until last Thursday."

Hodgins wrote in his notebook and flipped back

through the pages. *Drat*, he thought. *That's the day after the body was found.* When he looked up at Richardson, he noticed a knowing smirk on the man's face. Hodgins slammed his notebook closed and shoved it in his overcoat pocket. "That's all I need for now."

Hodgins turned his back on Richardson and started back to the train station. He thought he heard Richardson laughing, but wasn't going to turn around to check. He cursed most of the way along the street. He wasn't paying any attention to where he was going and collided with someone coming out of the post office.

"Oaf. Watch where you're going."

Hodgins mumble an apology and picked up the package the man dropped. He froze when he saw it was Flanagan.

"Oh, it's you again," Flanagan said. "I hope you aren't here to harass me or my family."

"No, Mr. Flanagan. Just checking a few things. Sorry to have disturbed you." Hodgins handed the package to Flanagan then realized he'd turned the wrong way when he left the sawmill. He backtracked, hurrying to get to the train station. Richardson was not likely the killer. If he left Peterborough to go to Toronto, he would definitely have been missed. Much as Hodgins wanted to arrest the man, he didn't have cause. And now he'd ruffled Flanagan's feathers. Hodgins had found out a few new minor details; nothing particularly helpful. The frustration he felt made him more determined then ever to find out who killed Fred Walker.

CHAPTER 12

Hodgins knew he was late for church, but he took his time brushing the lint from his suit jacket. He want to look his best. He gave the front of the jacket one final stroke. Something crinkled. He put the brush on the dressing table, and reached into the pocket.

"Oh, forgot all about you," he said. The letter that had been delivered to the station on Friday remained unopened.

"Hurry up Bertie," Cordelia called from the bottom of the staircase. "I don't care to be late again. Mother is already quite upset."

Hodgins placed the envelope beside the clothes brush and put his jacket on while rushing down the stairs.

His father-in-law had hired a carriage for the day as the temperature had dropped well below freezing. His mother-in-law glared at him all the way to the church. Bertie had been thinking of moving more and more the past several weeks. He leaned over Sara and whispered to

Cordelia.

"We need to talk later today." She started to say something, but he shook his head. "Later."

They arrived at the Church of the Holy Trinity on Yonge Street about five minutes before the service started and slid into an empty pew. Hodgins barely had time to sit when he felt a tap on his shoulder. He turned and faced the man who ran the haberdashery.

"Bin reading about that lad what was killed by the lake. Saw your name in the paper. Know who dun it?"

"Still investigating. We'll have the man responsible soon."

Several people hushed them and Hodgins turned back as the minister approached the pulpit. Hodgins didn't hear any of the service. He couldn't stop thinking about Flanagan and Richardson and was startled when Cordelia nudged him and told him to hush. He had a habit of mumbling when trying to sort out details, but had never done it in church before.

He tried listening to the end of the service, but was distracted by someone two rows up snoring. Sara clasped both hands over her mouth to hide her giggles; Hodgins put his arm around her shoulder. She looked up at him and he put one finger over his mouth and winked. Fortunately the choir started singing Holy, Holy, Holy, and drowned out her soft laugh.

Cordelia's father insisted on treating everyone for lunch after church, so it was late afternoon before Hodgins had a chance to speak with his wife alone. She sat on the bed waiting patiently while Hodgins paced across the room. "What is it Bertie? You've been acting strange all day. You're starting to scare me."

He stopped pacing and blurted it out. "I think it's time for us to move."

Cordelia was stunned. "Move? But why Bertie? I don't understand." She got up and walked to the window. "I love this house. I grew up here. I can't imagine living anywhere else." She turned to face him. "It's mother, isn't it? I'll speak to her."

"No. Well, maybe partly." He walked to Cordelia and took her hands in his.

"I'm grateful to your parents. They took me in when my folks died. I don't know what I would have done without them. Moved out west to live with my brother and his wife most likely. Everything had to be sold to pay the bills. I was left with nothing. No money for the rest of law school. No home. Nothing, except you. We couldn't have afforded to get married without their generosity. Then Sara came along. I've lived off their charity for over ten years."

He dropped her hands and turned away from her. "I

feel like I've failed you. It's time for me to support my wife and child."

Cordelia slipped her arms around his waist and laid her head against his shoulder.

"Oh Bertie. You haven't failed us. I had no idea you felt this way. If you want to move, we'll move. I suppose it's time for me to change too. Time to stop being a daughter and become more of a wife and mother. I don't care if we live in a tiny flat. As long as we're together."

He patted her hands. "Don't worry. I've been saving all these years. We can afford a house. Not quite this extravagant, but big enough."

Hodgins freed himself from Cordelia's grip and pulled her around to face him. "We won't struggle. You'll see."

Cordelia knew her mother would be devastated to learn Sara would be leaving. She was very attached to her grand-daughter. Cordelia reached for the chair at the dressing table and sat down. "What will I tell mother?"

Hodgins shrugged as he spotted the envelope sitting on the table. He walked over and picked it up.

"What's that?" she asked. "Is that blood?"

"Mine. Sliced my finger when I started to open it. It was delivered to the station on Friday. I get interrupted every time I try to read it."

"Well, there's no interruptions now."

Hodgins flipped open the envelope and pulled out a single sheet of paper. The message was short.

"Well? What does it say?"

"Hmm? What? Oh, nothing." Hodgins didn't look up from the letter.

"Nothing my Aunt Fanny." Cordelia reached out and grabbed it from his hand. "Oh dear heaven. Bertie, please tell me this is a joke."

"I don't think it is. I must be getting close. Wish I knew which direction to go." He took the letter back and read it one more time. Letters had been cut from a newspaper and pasted to the page.

DROP THE WALKER CASE

OR PAY THE PRICE.

CHAPTER 13

Hodgins rose the next morning, a little groggy. He dragged himself out of bed and got dressed for another day of work. He walked over to the dressing table, picked up the envelope, and stuffed it back into his jacket pocket. *Is it a real threat, or is someone just trying to scare me?*

He cursed himself for allowing Cordelia to read it. He wasn't worried, but his wife had been jumpy all last evening, and her parents noticed. When she broke a dish after dinner, she told them she was just tired. Hodgins knew lying to her parents added to Cordelia's unease, and that infuriated him more than the letter. This morning they were both tired due to her tossing and turning all night. He was even more motivated to solve the case and put it behind him.

His mood lifted slightly as he caught a whiff of breakfast. He hurried down the stairs and into kitchen where Cordelia was preparing eggs, toast and sausages. He could already taste her homemade preserves. Early morning was his favourite time to relax alone with his wife. It was the only time the house was quiet as no one else was up.

Hodgins pulled one of the chairs from the table and guided his wife into it. "Don't fret so. It's just a hollow threat. Stop fussing and sit down." Feeling guilty for worrying her, he served his wife breakfast before sitting down with a plate of his own. Cordelia always had one hardboiled egg, one piece of toast, and a little jelly. Occasionally she had a sausage as a bit of a treat. Hodgins had a plate full of scrambled eggs, three or four sausages, and two pieces of toast drowning in Cordelia's peach jelly.

Cordelia pushed her plate away. "Bertie, what if it's real? Can't someone else take over?

Hodgins put his hand over hers and smiled. "It doesn't work that way Delia. Believe me, there's nothing to worry about. Now eat something." He put her plate back in front of her, picked up her fork and placed it in her hand. "Eat. You'll need your strength when Sara wakes. You'll be running around trying to get her ready for school."

Cordelia nodded. "I supposed you're right. She does take it out of me in the mornings."

She ate a few bites of toast while Hodgins quickly cleared his plate.

"I do love your peach jelly," he said, and popped the last bite of toast into his mouth.

She poured him a cup of tea.

"No time. You take it. Sit, enjoy the quiet while you can." He kissed her and hurried out to catch the trolley.

Even though the sun had been up for a few hours, it was gloomy and cold. The dark clouds filling the sky indicated a storm was on its way. Hodgins was glad the trolley was crowded and wedged himself into the centre to hide from the wind. By the time he arrived at the station house his protective human wall had thinned, and he was wishing he'd had that cup of steaming hot tea before leaving.

As he stepped off the trolley he heard something. Looking around, he caught a glimpse of movement at the corner of the building. He supposed it was the stray dog. The crate one of the men had turned into a bed for it had been placed at the end of the alley, out of the way of the wind. The crate was also near the side door making it easy to sneak food out. The dog must be looking for handouts again. He walked into the alley to check on the mutt. Two men waited in the shadows.

"Is there a problem men?" Hodgins inquired.

One of the men stepped out of the darkness, holding something in front of his face so Hodgins couldn't tell who it was. Before Hodgins could say anything a burlap sack covered his head. Someone grabbed his arms and held them behind his back.

"Guess ya thought the note was a joke." Hodgins didn't recognize the gruff voice. "Maybe ya'll listen to this."

The blow to Hodgins stomach was unexpected and hard. He started to double over but the man behind him jerked him upright.

"This is fer sticking yer nose where it don't got no business bein'."

The next blow landed on his jaw. Hodgins could taste blood. Blow after blow followed. First the right side, then the left. Over and over. Blood ran into his mouth, mixed with bits of burlap. He tried to call for help, but only a gurgle came out. Hodgins managed to kick the man punching him, but it didn't slow him down. He became lightheaded.

"Who -" Hodgins started to ask.

The assault to his face stopped, but the relief was only temporary. One hard punch into his kidneys had him doubling over again. The man behind him let go. Hodgins hit the ground. Both men kicked him repeatedly. Hodgins felt a sharp pain in his side, then passed out.

Hodgins woke to the sound of barking. He was

groggy and shook his head to try to clear it. The wave of nausea almost made him pass out again. He managed to sit upright and tried to look around. Everything was dark. The barking stopped. He felt something wet on his face. Reaching out he felt fur. The smell told him it was probably the station's stray. He moved his hands across his face, wincing at the pain. His eyes felt huge. They were swollen shut. The dog barked again. Louder and louder.

"Quiet down boy," a voice called from the far end of the alley. The dog howled and whimpered, and then barked continually.

Hodgins heard footsteps hurrying towards him.

"Move along," the voice said. Go sober up somewhere else or I'll have ta lock ya up."

Hodgins recognized the voice. "Harrington," he whispered. He felt a hand on his shoulder.

"Lord Jesus," Harrington said. "Detective Hodgins."

Hodgins felt an arm slip under his. "I'll help you inside. Can you stand?"

With the help of the constable, Hodgins got to his feet and slowly made his way down the alley and in through the back door. The next few hours were hazy as he slipped in and out of consciousness. He could hear voices and someone in the distance called for a nurse. He figured he was at the hospital, but his eyes were still swollen shut. There was a tightness around his head. He touched his head and felt gauze. A bandage was wrapped around, covering his eyes.

"How do you feel, Sir?"

"Barnes, is that you?"

"Yes, Sir. We were all worried. Who knows how long you'dve been laying there if it weren't for the dog."

"The dog? I remember the barking and the dirty thing licking me."

"If he hadn't been making such a fuss we wouldn't have known you were there. He may have saved your life." Barnes hesitated before continuing in a lowered voice. "Few of us chipped in and got the mutt a nice piece of beef, sort of reward."

Hodgins chuckled. "Might just do that myself." He licked his lips. "Is there any water?"

He heard footstep, the sound of water pouring, then more footsteps.

"Here. The nurse brought in a jug while you were sleeping." Barnes touched the glass against one of Hodgins' hands. He clasped it tight. His hands were shaking as he raised it to his mouth. Empting it in one long gulp, he held it out for Barnes to take.

"Thank you. Don't supposed they'd let me have a cup of tea?"

"Probably not," Barnes replied as he took the glass.

Hodgins listened as the constable walked back to the table to return the empty class.

"What time is it?"

"A little past two, Sir."

"Two? I've been out half the day. Does my wife know?"

"Not yet. I was waiting for you to come to. They gave you something to help you sleep. What happened? Who did this?"

Hodgins shrugged. "Didn't see. They were in the shadows and put a burlap bag over my head. Think one of them had an Irish brogue. Can you go fetch my father-in-law? I don't want Cordelia to see me like this. We'll talk tomorrow."

"Yes, Sir." Barnes turned to leave.

"Barnes, my suit jacket. Is it here?"

Barnes looked around. "Yes, it's on the chair."

"There's a letter in the pocket. Take it back to the station."

Barnes went over to the coat, found the letter and read it. He whistled. "Sir? - "

"Tomorrow Barnes. Now go."

CHAPTER 14

Hodgins spent the next three days in the Toronto General Hospital. The doctor had to wait for the swelling in Hodgins' eyes to go down enough to allow him to check for damage. His examination showed the impression of what appeared to be a ring beside Hodgins' right eye. Fortunately the only damage to his left eye was a slight scratch to the iris, possibly from the burlap.

The doctor was concerned with the blood in Hodgins' urine, and wouldn't release him until the colour changed from red to light pink and there was no more pain when he pressed on Hodgin's kidney.

Cordelia came to the hospital each day after Sara went to school fussing and fretting over Hodgins' bedside. After the first day, he started feigning sleep, and even asked the nurse for a sleeping tablet.

Friday morning Cordelia and her father arrived at the hospital in a rented carriage to take Hodgins home. He was glad to finally be leaving the hospital, but was not looking forward to being fussed over all day by his overly concerned wife.

When the carriage stopped in front of the house, Hodgins struggled to get out. The bumpy ride had been more then he could endure and he desperately wanted some of the pain tablets the doctor has prescribed. With the help of Harold, he was able to get up the stairs and into bed. Sara ran into the room and was about to leap onto the bed when her mother grabbed her.

"Your father needs rest. Come down to the kitchen. We'll make something special for him. Would you like that?"

"Oh yes. We'll make Daddy some of grandmother's special chicken soup. That will make him all better." Sara ran past Cordelia and down the stairs.

"Is there anything I can do for you?" she asked.

"My tablets. Where are they?"

Cordelia took a small packet out her beaded reticule and handed him one tablet. He swallowed it without waiting for a glass of water. She tucked the quilt around him and went downstairs with her father.

"He'll be fine Cordelia. Try not to worry."

* * *

Over the next few days Cordelia was constantly hovering over him. She was staring at him every time he woke. With help, Hodgins was able to come down and sit in the front room where he chatted with his father-in-law, read the paper, or dozed by the fire.

The mixture of sympathy and fear was too much for him to take. He felt vulnerable and helpless. The inspector had told him to take as much time as he needed, but Hodgins was restless and frustrated sitting around doing nothing. He also was getting very tired of those looks from Cordelia's mother. He never realized just how annoying a simple 'titch' could be. Once he had the Walker case solved, he was going to start looking for a house.

Three days in the hospital and five days at home was all he could take. Sara was the only person who seemed unaffected. "You look funny, Daddy. Does it hurt?" He was glad she was too young to understand.

Nine days after the beating he was finally back at work. The young, new constables seemed afraid to talk for fear of saying something wrong. Some were shocked seeing a seasoned officer so badly beaten, and right outside the police station. The older officers made jokes. At least no one was fussing over him.

Hodgins sat at his desk and called Barnes over. He'd given Barnes a list of things to check and people to speak to earlier in the week when he came over to check on Hodgins' progress. Barnes sat in the chair opposite

Hodgins and put his notebook on the table.

"Shall I get us both a cup of tea?" Before Hodgins could reply, Barnes scurried to the back room and returned with two cups, then settled down with his notebook. Hodgins was glad to see the lad beginning to show some confidence.

"I sent a wire to the police in Peterborough. They spoke to Richardson's sister and she confirmed he was there the entire time. He was never away for any lengthy period, except to pick up supplies at the store and someone went with him. I believe we can scratch him off the list."

Hodgins slammed his fist on the desk, rattling the tea cups. "Damn. I was hoping you could find a hole in his story." He took a gulp of tea and waved his hand at Barnes, indicating he should continue.

"I went back to the wharf and spoke to anyone working near Flanagan's deserted building. One person recalls seeing someone go into the building, but he was too far away to see him good, and he only caught a glimpse."

"No," Hodgins said. "It would be too convenient for someone to have seen him. Wouldn't want our job made easy, would we?"

The puzzled look on Barnes' face let Hodgins know his sarcasm was wasted. "Go on."

"I went back to the empty building and walked up to the road. You know, where the footprints led."

Hodgins nodded.

"Spoke to some of the merchants again. A couple of them remembered seeing a man in his forties or fifties. Well dressed. He didn't stop at any of the businesses, so they didn't pay much attention."

Hodgins yawned, closed his eyes and leaned back in his chair. After a few moments he realized Barnes had stopped talking. He opened his eyes and saw Barnes drinking his tea, waiting.

"Sorry. Guess I'm still a little groggy from the tablets the doctors gave me."

He sat up, and pushed away from his desk. "Maybe another cup of tea will help."

Barnes jumped up and reached for Hodgins cup. "I'll get it."

Hodgins slapped Barnes' hand. "Sit down. The walk will help clear my head." He leaned over and looked at Barnes' cup. "I'll top up yours, too."

Hodgins came back with two steaming cups, each with a scone on the saucer. "The sergeant's wife did some baking for us again." He placed one cup in front of Barnes and sat down with his. "So, basically you're telling me we have nothing?"

117

It was Barnes' turn to nod.

"We've been over this time and again," Hodgins said. "There must be something we've overlooked. Someone must have said something that just wasn't right." He drummed his fingers on the desk. "Maybe we're looking at this all wrong. I've assumed it had something to do with Emily Flanagan. We never looked any further into Walker's background.

Hodgins flipped open his notebook and found a fresh page. He jotted down points as he talked. "We knew he was close to Emily Flanagan back in England, he had a fight with John Richardson, and an altercation with Patrick Flanagan." He looked up at Barnes.

"We don't know anything about him after he came to Canada. Could something have happened in those few years that lead to his death?" He sighed, "Another train ride to Stouffville. I wish there was another way to talk to him. Wouldn't it be nice if we could just push a button and talk to someone in another location? Guess that will never happen." He chuckled at the thought.

"I need to have another talk with his cousin and I don't want to wait until the weekend when he's at home. Send him a telegram and tell him I'll be taking the early evening train tomorrow."

* * *

Hodgins stomped his feet, and shook his overcoat to remove the snow before stepping inside. "Thank you for seeing me tonight, Mr. Lowe."

"Anything to speed this up," Lowe replied. "Not to be rude, but what happened to your face?"

"Little altercation a week or so ago. Believe it or not it looks much better now. Hazard of the job I'm afraid."

"Yes, I suppose it is. Do you have news? I'm anxious to find out who killed my cousin." He took Hodgins' coat and hung it on a peg by the door, then led him into the drawing room. Two chairs had been moved close to the fireplace. Hodgins welcomed the warmth as a storm had started while he was on the train. Before Lowe closed the door, Hodgins could hear the sounds of happy chattering and clinking dishes coming from the back of the house. He guessed Mr. Lowe had not informed his wife of the telegram or visit, or she would be sitting with them.

Lowe sat in the chair opposite Hodgins and fidgeted with the sleeve of his jacket. "What can I do for you, Detective?"

Hodgins thought for a moment. He didn't want to make his questions sound like he though Fred had done something to deserve being murdered.

"Tell me about Mr. Walker's arrival in Canada."

Mr. Lowe relaxed a little. "Fred was twenty-two.

Didn't know a soul. My father brought us over years earlier so I hadn't seen Fred since he was a toddler. We were practically strangers."

Lowe got a far-away look in his eyes. "Fred was rather shy at first, but we soon became close. He told me about Emily. Got the impression they were inseparable. I think he missed her more than he missed his father. He settled in quick enough though. My family had a farm just outside town. He shared a room with his little brother and me. His sister bunked in with my sister. I had just become engaged and married less than a year later. Fred came over to visit often, and I helped him get the job at the mill."

"So, nothing of consequence happened in the past, what, four years? No problems, no sweethearts?"

Lowe smiled. "Fred was young, good looking, single, and new. He was popular with the young ladies and in demand at the dances. He got over his shyness right quick."

"And he came to live here after your parents died?"

"Yes. Father passed away shortly after Fred arrived, and my sister married last year and moved to New York. Mother died shortly after. We sold the farm and took in Fred.

"I see. Fred had no problems? Not even minor ones?"

"No, nothing until that altercation with John Richardson last fall."

"Right." Hodgins slapped the cover of his notebook closed. The flames in the fireplace flickered as a gust of wind whistled down the chimney.

"I have a few more people to talk to before heading back to the train station. It sounds like it's getting worse outside. If you remember anything, no matter how trivial, please contact me right away."

Hodgins bundled up and headed into the snow storm. He wanted to speak with Miss. Cooke. Barnes was so enamoured with her Hodgins was not entirely confident the interview was complete. Unfortunately she wasn't able to provide any further information, so he headed back to the train station to wait for the last train out. He cursed in frustration the entire way, and barely noticed how cold it was.

CHAPTER 15

Hodgins was distracted all through supper. He normally enjoyed Cordelia's mutton; it was a rare treat. She always took care to make the entire meal extra special whenever they ate it. But Hodgins could have been eating boiled socks that evening and he wouldn't have noticed the difference. There was something about the Walker case he couldn't put his finger on. Something was telling him he had the proof, but he didn't know what it was.

When the meal was over he mumbled an apology and went straight up to his room. He paced back and forth for awhile, then stood looking out the window. An hour later the bedroom door slammed, breaking his concentration and causing him to jump.

"How could you be so rude?" Cordelia asked. "Mother is in a state and Sara is extremely upset. She thinks she did something wrong and is nearly in tears."

"Rude? Was I?" Hodgins hurried across the room

and put his arms around his wife. "I'm sorry. I'm just so distracted with this case. I'll go talk to Sara soon."

Cordelia pulled away from him. "I'm frightened. In all the years you've been a police officer this is the first time you've been so badly hurt. When I first saw you at the hospital I thought I was going to lose you." Her lower lip quivered. "I didn't know what to tell Sara."

"I didn't realize it was affecting you so." Hodgins reach towards Cordelia.

She stomped her foot. "No. You can't make it go away with an embrace. I'm frightened and angry, and nothing you do or say will change that. All those trips to Stouffville, and now this." She lightly touched his bruised face and took a deep breath. The tension left her body. "When we married, I always thought the day might come when another officer came to the door. I accepted that. Now I have to deal with it. At least you came home – this time."

She forced a tiny smile. "Now, tell me what you've discovered and get this murder solved once and for all."

Hodgins kissed Cordelia on the forehead, then retrieved his notebook from his desk and sat down.

"I've only had two good suspects. Patrick Flanagan and John Richardson. Barnes confirmed Richardson's alibi, so that leaves Flanagan. Problem is, I don't have anything to tie him to the murder."

Cordelia walked over to the desk and stood beside him. "What about the cufflink?"

Hodgins sighed. "Ah yes. The pearl cufflink. I haven't the foggiest notion whose it is. It may not even have anything to do with Walker."

He banged his fist on the desktop. "Blast. This is so frustrating." The pages of his notebook fluttered from the breeze his fist caused. They settled at the spot where he had copied the sketch of the bruise on the back of Walker's head.

Cordelia giggled and pointed. "What about your little birdie?"

Hodgins laughed. "That is the most peculiar bruise I've ever seen. Haven't figured that out either. What in tarnation would leave a mark like that?"

Cordelia patted his shoulder. "I'm sure I don't know, Dear. Can't the local police in Stouffville help?"

"No local police. It's a small town and there isn't much crime.

Hodgins closed the notebook and got up. "I'd better speak to Sara before she goes to bed."

* * *

His previous evening's chat with Cordelia left Hodgins with a strong feeling he was on the right track. Something about that darn bruise. He spent a restless night trying to piece it all together, rising early to allow his wife the luxury of sleeping late. He grabbed a couple of thick slices of bread and piled some peach preserves on them. The trolley was practically empty so he had no trouble finding a seat to eat his breakfast without making a mess.

He stepped off the trolley and strode towards the station. He hesitated when he reached the alley. Hodgins watched the shadows, ensuring no-one was lurking. Satisfied, he continued to the front steps. He took one quick look around before entering the building.

Hodgins walked past the desk sergeant, mumbled a 'Good Morning' and went straight to the back for a cup of tea. The stationhouse was quiet and he could hear the gentle snoring of one of the senior constables. A sure sign of an evening free of trouble.

Hodgins put the tea cup on his desk and removed his notebook as he walked to the coat tree to hang his overcoat. He opened the book to look for the first notes on the Walker case as he ambled back to his desk. Pulling a pad of long paper from the top drawer he copied what he figured were the key points, along with his thoughts about them. He had three pages filled by the time Barnes came in.

"Do you have new information?" Barnes asked.

Without waiting to be asked he sat in the chair opposite Hodgins' desk. His eyes were wide, eagerly awaiting good news.

The reply was curt. "No." Hodgins put his pencil down and started drumming his fingers. "It's here. I know it is." He fanned the pages of foolscap. "The answer is in here – somewhere."

"What's that there?" Barnes pointed to a few words that Hodgins had circled.

Hodgins picked up his notebook and found the page with the notes from the autopsy and pointed to the sketch. "It's this damn bruise. My wife noticed that it's shaped like a bird." He turned the book around. "See?"

Barnes leaned in for a closer look. "Well, look at that. Is it important?"

Hodgins shrugged. "Not sure. I think so, but I can't for the life of me figure out what made it. If we can determine that, we'll probably have the killer. Whatever it was that made that mark, there can't be too many of them."

He tapped the circled notes on the pad of paper. "These two things are crucial, I just know it." He turned the pad so Barnes could read it.

"The bruise and the pearl cufflink." Barnes looked up at Hodgins. "Did you find out who owns the cufflink?"

Hodgins sighed, "No."

"Another train ride to Stouffville?" Barnes asked.

Hodgins nodded. "Yes, but not today. I need to have a plan. The only way to solve this will be to catch them off guard. If they think I know something one of them may slip up."

"Makes sense. I've used that trick on my younger brother lots of times." Barnes said. "He was so gullible." He smiled. "Still is."

"Somehow I doubt Flanagan is easily fooled. I'll need you to come with me. Might be more believable if it appears as though I brought help, anticipating an arrest." He glanced over at the calendar on the wall. "January thirtieth. It's been just over three weeks since those boys found Mr. Walker's body. Tomorrow is Saturday. Month end. If I'm any judge of character, Flanagan will be out early collecting rent from those properties he lets out. We'll take the first train after lunch tomorrow. He should be home by then."

CHAPTER 16

Hodgins and Barnes purchased return tickets and boarded the one o'clock train Saturday afternoon, hoping to surprise Flanagan at home.

There were a large number of people scattered throughout the coach cars, most laden with parcels, returning from an early morning shopping trip. Hodgins made his way to an empty window seat and Barnes slid in beside him. Hodgins was still trying to figure out the key piece that continued to elude him, ignoring Barnes' attempts to engage him in conversation.

As the train travelled through the countryside, Hodgins stared out the window. The length of track between Toronto and Stouffville was thick with pine and spruce trees covered in snow. He didn't pay any attention as people departed and boarded at each stop along the way. Blue Jays called and screeched from the woods beside the tracks, and when Barnes pointed them out Hodgins slapped his arm down. Jackrabbits hopped out from under the trees and Red Tailed Hawks circled about, but Hodgins ignored it all.

Barnes frequently looked up from the newspaper he'd purchased at Union Station and tried unsuccessfully to draw Hodgins' attention to the picturesque scene outside. By the time the train pulled into Stouffville, Hodgins was still no wiser than when he had boarded.

As they walked to the Smythe's house, Hodgins fiddled with the collar of his overcoat. The wind had died down and he no longer needed it up around his neck. Barnes loosened the brightly coloured scarf he had wound around his throat and tucked inside his coat.

"Where did you get that thing?" Hodgins asked.

"My mother knit it for me for Christmas. It's quite warm."

"Oh, it's very . . . colourful."

They reached the Smythe house and approached the front door. Hodgins looked at Barnes, crossed his fingers, and knocked.

Mr. Smythe answered the door. He recognized the detective immediately. "Yes, what it is now?"

"I'd like to speak with Mr. Flanagan if he's home."

Smythe stepped back and gestured for Hodgins and Barnes to come in. "It's not about that business with young Fred, is it? Patrick told you everything before."

They stepped into the house and closed the door. "There have been some new developments. Won't take long. Is he in?"

Mr. Smythe looked past Hodgins at Barnes. "This is one of my constables. I thought it prudent to bring him along," Hodgins said.

Smythe glared at the detective, then snorted lightly. "Make it quick. My wife will be home soon and I'd rather you weren't here when she returns. Wait in the drawing room and I'll fetch Patrick."

Smythe ushered Hodgins and Barnes into the drawing room. Barnes remained by the door, acting like a guard, making it appear as though they knew more than they actually did. Hodgins walked over to the fireplace to admire the new family portrait that now hung over the mantle when a commotion in the hall caught his attention. The door opened and Flanagan entered, his wife, Emily was right on his heels followed by her father. Barnes reached over and closed the door.

Flanagan turned to his wife. "Emily, this is a not a discussion you need to be concerned with."

"Fred was my friend, a long time friend. I have every right to know what's going on." She crossed her arms and turned away from her husband. "I'm staying, and that's that."

Emily marched across the drawing room, sat on the edge of one of the chairs near the fire and looked anxiously at Hodgins. "Detective, Daddy said there was some new information. Do you know who killed Fred?"

"I just need to clear up a few details. He turned to Flanagan and pulled the pearl cufflink from his pocket.

Hodgins held his hand out towards Flanagan. "Do you recognize this?

Flanagan looked at the cufflink in Hodgins' hand. "I have a pair like that. Why?"

"When was the last time you wore them?"

"I don't know. Last fall possibly. I believe I wore them to the local businessmen's banquet in November."

"You didn't wear them around Christmas?"

Flanagan's face turned red. "I just said I haven't worn them for months. What are you getting at?"

Emily rose to get a better look at the cufflinks. "That does look like the pair you have." she said. "Daddy borrowed them for a meeting in Toronto just a few weeks ago." She turned her head towards her father. "Isn't that right Daddy?"

"What?" Smythe said. "Well, yes. I suppose I did."

Hodgins flipped the cufflink in his hand. He looked from Smythe to Flanagan and back to Smythe. "You wore the cufflinks last? Where are they now?"

Smythe shook his head. "I guess I gave them back to Emily."

Hodgins turned his attention to Emily.

"Yes, that's correct. I remember Daddy giving the box back and putting it on the dressing table. It was just last week I believe."

Hodgins caught a slight movement out of the corner of his eye. He turned his head just enough to get a better look without being noticed.

Smythe was looking at Emily and shaking his head, but she was looking at Hodgins.

"Just last week?" Hodgins asked. "He didn't return them right away?"

Emily shrugged. "I guess he forgot."

"And you're sure this is not one of your husband's cufflinks?"

"How could it be? It is very similar to his though. Patrick's very proud of them. Genuine pearls and 24k gold. He was livid when Harry, my little brother, damaged one of them. Left a mark on one of the bars. The gold is rather soft."

"Would you mind fetching them?" Hodgins asked.

"Of course." Emily hurried upstairs and returned shortly with a small red velvet box. "Here they are," she said as she entered the room. She opened the box. "That's odd." Emily took one cufflink from the box and dropped it in Hodgins' hand next to the other one.

"These aren't Patrick's."

"What do you mean?" Hodgins asked.

"The one you brought is very good quality. You can see the color of the gold doesn't match this one. The pair I have are probably only 10k, not 24k."

Emily took the cufflink back from Hodgins and turned it over several times, then did the same with its mate. "There's no mark on them either. Someone must have replaced Patrick's with these cheap copies."

Hodgins examined the cufflink that was found by the body. "Hmm." He ran his fingers across the bar then showed it to Emily. "Is this the mark that your brother made?"

"It looks like it. That's the same place it was damaged." She looked up at Hodgins. "How did you get it?"

Hodgins looked behind Emily at Patrick. "It was found beside Mr. Walker's body."

Everyone turned toward Flanagan. Barnes took a few steps into the room.

"I don't know how my cufflink ended up with Walker's body." Sweat broke out across his forehead. "I didn't kill him. You've got to believe me." He took a hanky from his trousers pocket and swiped at his brow. "Why would I? I already had Emily. He was no threat to me, and my father-in-law had them last." He paused for a moment. "When exactly was he killed?"

"The coroner couldn't say, but it was the first week of January, maybe the fourth or fifth," Hodgins said.

"Well," Flanagan said. "That proves it. I haven't been to Toronto since the end of December. I was planning on making the trip this coming Monday to conduct some business."

"Can anyone vouch for you?" Hodgins asked.

"I'm sure my wife would be more than happy to." Flanagan turned to his wife.

"Emily, tell the detective I haven't left town all month." He waited. "Emily?"

Everyone's attention was directed at her, but she was examining the cufflinks she'd brought downstairs.

Flanagan reached out and placed a hand on her shoulder, causing her to jump.

"Tell him I've been in town all month."

Emily looked at her husband as though he was a stranger. "But how . . ."

Flanagan's neck turned red. "Emily! Tell the detective I have not left town for weeks."

Slowly she turned her head towards Hodgins, her eyes

still on her husband. Finally, she looked at the detective.

"Patrick has not been gone for more than two hours at any one time. He's been keeping an eye on the men working on the house."

"That's right," Mr. Smythe said. "I was with him on some of the visits to his house. I'm an architect. He hired me to draw up the plans."

This was not going the way Hodgins had hoped. He walked towards the fireplace, glanced up at it and turned. He got half way across the room and stopped. He looked at Smythe and turned back to the portrait hanging over the fireplace.

"Nice portrait. It wasn't here at my last visit. That's an interesting walking stick you're holding in the painting."

Smythe puffed out his chest and smiled. "It was a gift from my employees when we left Norfolk."

"They must have though highly of you to give you such an expensive looking thing."

"Yes," Smythe replied. "My business was small, and my staff was like a second family. They knew I would be giving up my hobby when I moved, so they got it as a reminder. I had a good sized piece of land and was able to keep a few falcons. I'm afraid I'm unable to keep the birds here. Shame. Falconry is such a thrilling sport. Such beautiful creatures."

Hodgins remember the odd shaped bruise the coroner mentioned. He walked over to Barnes and whispered to him. Barnes nodded. Hodgins turned back to Mr. Smythe. "Why did you do it Sir?"

"Pardon me? Do what?"

"Why did you murder him? At first I thought it was your son-in-law, but the walking stick was the final piece I was missing. What harm did Walker ever do to you?"

"You're mad. Daddy would never do such a thing." Emily rushed to her father's side and wrapped her arms around his waist. Smythe put his arm over her shoulder.

"This is absurd. Why would you think I did it?" Smythe turned to Emily. "Don't worry. It's all a mistake." He walked her to the chair by the fireplace and made her sit.

"You're just clutching at straws, Detective. I liked Fred. Why would I do such a horrible thing?"

Hodgins gestured towards Emily. "Your daughter just said you borrowed the cufflinks and went to Toronto a few weeks ago. When exactly was that?"

"It was the fifth. Monday afternoon. I was meeting with a new client. I can give you his name."

That won't be necessary. What time —"

Hodgins was interrupted by the slamming of the front door, followed by the giggling of a child. The drawing room door opened and a boy ran in, still wearing his snow-covered coat and boots.

"Harry!" Emily shouted.

The boy froze, and looked at everyone in the room. Mrs. Smythe hurried in after him.

"I'm sorry," she said. "Harry, you know better than that. Come here at once."

She noticed Hodgins. "You're that policeman, aren't you?"

Hodgins nodded.

Harry's mouth opened and his eyes grew large. "A real policeman?"

Hodgins smiled. "Yes, a real policeman. A detective."

Harry turned around and spotted Barnes. He walked over to Barnes and reached for one of the shiny brass buttons on his uniform.

"Harry, come here at once." Mrs. Smythe said.

The boy pouted and slowly followed her out into the front hall.

Hodgins watched closely as the boy walked past him and into the hall.

"Nice looking lad," he said. "I'd guess he'd be about four." He turned and looked at the boy again. "Hmm . . ." He took his notebook out of his pocket, flipped through the pages and pulled out the picture of Fred Walker. He looked at the picture again, then walked out into the hall and held the it beside the little boy's face. "Interesting."

Hodgins went back into the drawing room and showed Emily the picture of Fred.

"Can't help but notice how much Harry looks like Fred Walker."

Emily gasped and put her hand over her mouth.

Hodgins asked Barnes to close the door that Harry had left open.

"No," Emily said. She turned to her father. "Daddy, it's all for nothing. I married Patrick but everyone will still know."

"So, it's not a coincidence that the boy resembles Fred? Why marry that man and not the boy's father?" Hodgins asked, pointing at Flanagan.

"Blackmail," Smythe answered. "Fred had already moved when Emily found herself in a delicate condition. Once we knew, her mother took her on a tour of Europe. At least that's what we told folks. When they returned with the baby, we said it was ours. No one knew any difference." He glared at Emily. "Silly, stupid girl."

Emily covered her face with both hands and wept.

"Where does the blackmail come in?"

"When we moved here and Emily renewed her relationship with Fred, she started thinking about telling him. The boy is starting to look like his father, which you already discovered. If word got out, it would ruin her reputation, and the family name."

Hodgins looked at Emily. Her husband stood beside her chair, totally uninterested in her discomfort and distress. Puzzled, Hodgins turned his attention back to Smythe.

"But what does that have to do with Flanagan?" Hodgins asked Smythe.

"He showed up here one day with suggestions for some alterations to the drawings I did for his renovations." Smythe's eyes narrowed and he turned his head slightly towards Flanagan. "Quite rude if you ask me. I had gone upstairs to fetch the drawings and he overhead my wife and Emily talking about the boy. He had made several comments before so I knew he had an interest in Emily, but she wanted nothing to do with him. When I came back down he said if Emily didn't marry him, he would tell everyone about her indiscretion five years earlier."

"Buy why kill Mr. Walker," Hodgins asked.

Smythe stood tall. "I really don't know why you insist I did it."

"You had the cufflinks last, and one was found with the body. You noticed it was missing at some point. I'm sure it won't take long to find the jeweller who made the cheap copy. That's why you returned them to your daughter so late."

Smythe stood with his mouth open, the realization that he had been caught crept across his face. His shoulders dropped.

"I didn't plan to. Emily was still in love with Fred; I couldn't risk her leaving Patrick for him. It would all come out, and we would be ruined. This is a small, close knit community, and very religious. My wife and daughter would be shunned, and the men would stop doing business with me." Smythe glanced over at Emily. The look of horror on her face was more than he could bear.

"I bumped into Fred on the way to Union Station after my meeting. He suspected something and was hounding me to tell him why Emily married Patrick. We got into an argument. People were looking, so we moved off the road down near the wharf. He turned away from me and I hit him with the walking stick. I didn't mean to kill him, I just wanted him to stop asking questions."

"Where is it?" Hodgins asked. "The walking stick. I assume you still have it."

Smythe nodded. "Couldn't bear the thought of getting rid of it. It's in the stand by the front door."

Hodgins gestured to Barnes, who quickly went to the front door. He returned with the walking stick and handed it to Hodgins.

"There was a deep cut on his side," Hodgins said. He ran his fingers around the decorative carving on the top of the stick. It moved. Curious, Hodgins gently twisted and pulled. Attached to the carving was an eight inch blade.

"I was frantic." Smyth said. "I panicked and stabbed him after he fell."

Mr. Smythe held his arms out toward Barnes and said, "I won't cause any trouble." Barnes reached for his handcuffs.

"Put your arms down. I don't believe handcuffs will be necessary," Hodgins said.

"Thank you for that, Detective. If I plead guilty, there won't be a lengthy trial, will there? Could we keep the reason a secret? I don't want my family to suffer any more than they already will."

"Detective," Flanagan said. "You said it was the walking stick. I don't understand. What made you change your mind about me and suspect Emily's father?"

"It was the falcon on the top of the stick. Walker had a bruise on his head that looked like a bird. The shape resembles the one on the walking stick." He opened his notebook to the sketch of the bruise and showed Flanagan.

Hodgins turned back to Mr. Smythe. "If we leave

now we can catch the next train back to Toronto."

Emily started to cry. "Be brave Emily," her father said. "You must be strong for Mother and young Harry."

Hodgins opened the drawing room door and gestured for Barnes to escort Smythe.

"Just let me get my overcoat," Smythe said.

CHAPTER 17

Hodgins and Smythe walked towards the train station, Barnes followed close behind. Hodgins stopped on the platform to read the schedule printed on the chalkboard outside the waiting area. He checked his pocket watch. It would be twenty minutes before their train departed for Toronto, so they went inside to wait.

There was a bench near the pot belly stove; Hodgin's indicated for Smythe to sit, then sent Barnes to purchase a ticket for Smythe. They rested in silence listening to the sounds outside of the station: cattle mooing in the nearby pen waiting to be ushered to the slaughterhouse, the hissing of the engine that sat idling on the side rail, murmuring from travellers waiting for their train or for someone to arrive.

Hodgins looked over at the large round clock on the opposite wall. "May as well go outside and wait. Our train should be pulling in shortly." They got up and stood on the platform, near the doorway.

A stray dog was sniffing around looking for handouts. "Looks just like the mutt that hangs around the station house, except ours is much fatter. Everyone sneaks the poor bugger food. Last month one of the men made a shelter for it out of an old crate and tattered blanket." Hodgins smiled. "Even feed it myself, sometimes."

"Got no use for them myself," Smythe said. "Useless creatures. Always begging for food. They don't serve much purpose, if you ask me."

Hodgins thought back to the morning in the alley when he was attacked. "If you treat them right they know it. Might even save your life some day." He pointed down the platform at Hodgins. "See, my constable understands."

Barnes had a few crumbs of beef pie in his coat pocket, left over from a hasty lunch. He'd walked to the end of the platform towards the dog, crumbs held out in his hand. The dog's tail wagging as it cautiously approached. It sniffed at Barnes hands, then gently took the scraps of crust and beef. It gave a quiet bark, and wandered off searching for more food.

Smythe watched Barnes and snorted. "Disgusting, filthy mongrel. Your constable probably has fleas now. He'll spread them all over the train."

Hodgins held up his hand. "Hush. What's that sound?"

"Sound? What? That whistle? The train over there I expect."

"Doesn't sound right. I've never heard a train make that sound."

There was a loud boom, then yelling. A woman screamed; Hodgins blacked out.

* * *

When Hodgins opened his eyes, he was no longer at the train station.

"Nurse, he's awake," Barnes yelled.

"Barnes, is that you? Where am I?"

"In the hospital. You need to rest, Sir. So you can heal."

"Where's Smythe?"

"That's not important now. The doctor said you need lots of rest."

Hodgins started to sit up, wincing as the pain raged through his head. "Blast man, tell me what happened. Something happened at the station in Stouffville."

"Everyone's talking about it, Sir. The boiler of the Fairlie engine Shedden exploded. Seems the safety valves failed. Three of the enginemen were killed. The force sent you flying back against the wall. Knocked you out cold. Where is the nurse?"

Barnes hurried to the doorway and hollered, "Nurse,

doctor, someone. He's awake."

"That explains this headache," Hodgins said. "What about Smythe? Is he here too?"

Barnes turned back to Hodgins.

"Uh, no, Sir," Barnes said as he walked back to Hodgins bedside.

"Good Lord. Don't tell me he got away?"

"No. A piece of metal went straight though his heart. Was killed instantly."

Hodgins lay back in his hospital bed. "Well, I guess that saves Her Majesty the expense of a trial and hanging. Case closed."

Barnes stood at the foot of the bed, twirling his helmet in his hands. "Uh, Sir?"

Hodgins noticed Barnes fidgeting. "Yes?"

"What about the two men who attacked you? It was because of Walker's murder. Don't we still have to apprehend them before we can close the case?"

Hodgins closed his eyes, and waited for the pain to subside. "If we continue to investigate, we'll eventually have to reveal why Smythe did it, right?"

"Of course, Sir. We have to tell the truth. If we don't tell why, it's the same as a lie."

"What purpose will it serve to let everyone know that Emily Flanagan had a child out of wedlock when she was eighteen?"

"Well . . ." Barnes started.

"Do you want to ruin her life and that of the little boy?"

"No, of course not. But isn't it our duty to continue?"

Hodgins sighed. "I don't care who beat me up in the alley. Obviously Smythe hired them, so they have no reason to harm me again. It's our duty to solve crimes and capture the criminals. We've solved this murder, and the guilty party has paid with his life. No need to drag innocent people's names through the mud. It'll be difficult enough for them. Wouldn't be surprised if they moved away."

"Since you put it that way, then I guess we've done all we can." Barnes noticed Hodgins yawning. "I'll leave you to get some rest now, Sir."

Barnes turned to leave and bumped into the doctor.

"Terribly sorry, Doctor. Do excuse me."

The doctor said something under his breath and walked around Barnes.

Hodgins called out to Barnes. "Wait, I have something I need you to do."

EPILOGUE

After spending a few days in Toronto General, Hodgins was sent home to finish recuperating. He was glad to be home, where he wasn't being poked and examined constantly. Early Saturday morning everyone sat at the kitchen table finishing up breakfast when someone knocked at the front door.

"Who could be calling at such an early hour?" Cordelia asked as she rose from the table. "It's only just past 8:00. Early callers usually mean bad news."

Hodgins smiled. "Not necessarily. Answer it and you'll find out. Take Sara with you."

Cordelia put her hands on her hips. "Just what are you up to Bertie?"

He shrugged. "Why do you think I'm up to something? It's cold outside. Hurry, go answer the door before he freezes."

"Before who freezes?"

Cordelia's mother rose. "For goodness sake. I'll get

148

it."

Hodgins held out his hand. "No, sit. Let Cordelia and Sara get it."

Cordelia looked suspiciously at her husband. "Very well. Come on Sara. Let's go see what your father is up to."

Cordelia opened the front door and found Barnes standing on the porch. "Why hello, Constable. Come in and I'll call Bertie." She noticed a rope in his hand and followed it with her eyes. "What . . .?" She was confused. The constable was at their door, out of uniform, and with a dog.

"What's his name?" Sara asked. "Can I pat him?"

"Scraps." Barnes held out the rope for Sara to take. "He's right friendly, Miss, and loves to be petted." He stepped inside and closed the door behind him.

Hodgins came out of the kitchen with his in-laws, an agonized look clung to his face. His steps were guarded; he reached for the wall to steady himself. He was still rather wobbly from the explosion.

"Take your coat and boots off and come into the front room," Hodgins said. He popped one of his pain tablets into his mouth.

Cordelia glanced past her husband at her father, who shrugged. They hadn't been on social terms with the young constable, yet her husband was treating him like an old friend.

Sara led the dog into the front room and sat on the rug in front of the fire. Scraps curled up beside her, tail thumping against the floor.

Hodgins looked at the dog. Its coat was shiny and free of tangles. "Are you sure that's the same dog?"

"Yes, Sir. Cleaned up quite nice. Dr. McKenzie treated it for fleas and gave it a bath. Beautiful, ain't he?"

"Do you like him Sara?" Hodgins asked.

"Oh yes. He's very nice, and so soft." She turned to Barnes. "Why do you call him Scraps? Funny name for a dog."

Barnes smiled. "He was always hanging around the police station, and me and some of the boys fed him scraps of food. Seemed like an appropriate name for him, don't you think?"

Sara nodded and stroked the dog's fur. Scraps stood up, licked Sara's face, and lay down with his head in her lap.

"Is this the dog that found Bertie in the alley?" Cordelia asked.

"Yes, he's the one," Barnes answered.

Hodgins walked over to Barnes and shook his hand. "Thank you, Barnes."

"My pleasure, Sir. Least I could do."

Hodgins started to walk to the front door with Barnes.

"The dog. Don't forget the dog," Hodgins' mother-in-law called out.

The front door opened, then closed and Hodgins came back into the front room alone. "That's what this room was missing." He walked to the fireplace and knelt beside Sara and stroked the dog.

"Bertie?"

"I asked Barnes to catch and clean up the dog. I'm sure Sara will take good care of him. He did save my life after all."

ABOUT THE AUTHOR

Nanci M. Pattenden is a professional genealogist, and an author of historical crime fiction. Her interest in genealogy, local history and love of Victorian murder mysteries have merged to create a new Canadian Victorian murder mystery writer. She is a member of Crime Writers of Canada, The Writers Community of York Region, and the Ontario Genealogical Society.

She has completed the Creative Writing program at the University of Calgary, and has completed two programs with The Institute of Genealogical Studies (Canadian and English studies).

Nanci currently resides in Newmarket, Ontario with her diabetic cat.

nanci@nancipattenden.com
www.murderdoespayink.ca
www.nancipattenden.com
@alberthodgins
@npattenden

Printed in Great Britain
by Amazon